ZUBAAN-PENGUIN BOOKS

SHADOW MEN

Bijoya Sawian is a translator and writer who lives in Shillong and Dehradun. She is the author of several books including *The Teaching of Elders* and *Khasi Myths, Legends and Folktales*. This is her first novel.

SHADOW MEN

Bijoya Sawian

PENGUIN BOOKS

ZUBAAN
an imprint of Kali for Women
128 B Shahpur Jat, 1st floor
NEW DELHI 110 049
Email: zubaan@gmail.com and zubaanwbooks@vsnl.net. Website: www.zubaanbooks.com

In collaboration with

PENGUIN BOOKS
Published by the Penguin Group
Penguin Books India Pvt. Ltd, 11 Community Centre, Panchsheel Park,
New Delhi 110 017, India
Penguin Group (USA), 375 Hudson Street, New York, New York 10014, USA
(a division of Penguin Group (USA) Inc.)
Penguin Group (Canada), 90 Eglinton Avenue East, Suite 700, Toronto,
Ontario, M4P 2Y3, Canada (a division of Pearson Penguin Canada Inc.)
Penguin Group (UK), 80 Strand, London WC2R 0RL, England
(a division of Penguin Books Ltd)
Penguin Group (Ireland), 25 St Stephen's Green, Dublin 2, Ireland
(a division of Penguin Books Ltd)
Penguin Group (Australia), 250 Camberwell Road, Camberwell,
Victoria 3124, Australia (a division of Pearson Australia Group Pty Ltd)
Penguin Group (NZ), 67 Apollo Drive, Rosedale, North Shore 0632, New Zealand
(a division of Pearson New Zealand Ltd)
Penguin Group (South Africa), 24 Sturdee Avenue, Rosebank,
Johannesburg 2196, South Africa (a division of Penguin Group (South Africa) (pty) Ltd)

Penguin Books Ltd, Registered Offices: 80 Strand, London WC2R 0RL, England

First published by Penguin Books India and Zubaan Books 2010
Copyright © Bijoya Sawian 2010

All rights reserved
10 9 8 7 6 5 4 3 2 1

This is a work of fiction. Names, characters, places and incidents are either the product of the author's imagination or are used fictitiously and any resemblance to any actual person, living or dead, events or locales, is entirely coincidental.

ISBN 9788189884581

Typeset by RECTO Graphics, Delhi 110 096.
Printed at Yash Printographics, Noida.

This book is sold subject to the conditions that it shall not, by way or trade or otherwise, be lent, resold, hired out or otherwise circulated without the publisher's prior written consent in any form of binding or cover other than that in which it is published and without a similar condition including this condition being imposed on the subsequent purchaser and without limiting the rights under copyright reserved above, no part of this publication may be reproduced, stored in or introduced into a retrieval system, or transmitted in any form or by any means (electronic, mechanical, photocopying, recording or otherwise), without the prior written permission of both the copyright owner and the above-mentioned publisher of this book.

For

My English teacher

Mother Nives

and

Aneeta

Prologue

THEY SAY THAT when you are alive you are actually dreaming and when you die you awaken. That summer was like a dream with the wakefulness of life, that summer in the faraway hill town where I grew up long ago, so long ago it seems like a past life almost. There, among the vicissitudes of nature, I found myself dreaming a dream so frightening that it woke me forever.

1

GHOSTLIKE, THE MIST floated up from the gorge below, encircling the gardener's cottage and the trees, seeping languidly through the flowering shrubs. It climbed up the hedge of azaleas, and gently made its way past the tall monsoon grass. It parted slightly and I noticed three figures climbing up the west-facing slope. Something about the way they moved caught my eye. It wasn't the easy, after-work saunter of household staff. They were quick and furtive, yet clumsy and clearly unfamiliar with the terrain and the path that zigzagged through the plum and peach orchard.

The mist thickened, now rising quickly to form an impenetrable curtain. And then, suddenly, it broke to expose the three young men, now in the dimly lit verandah of the cottage next door. One of them had a gun. Rooted to the ground and cold with fright I watched his sinister silhouette.

The other two were leaning against the wooden posts that shouldered the leaky tin roof of the verandah. The man with the gun went into the cottage. His companions looked around with an air of seeming nonchalance. I thought that one of them had a face blotchy with white leucoderma patches, but I couldn't be sure. Just at that moment, the telephone rang.

2

"HELLO!"

"Hi! Is that you Raseel?"

"Yes…"

"Hi! Why, why are you sounding so distant? Don't you recognize my voice? Can't you hear me?"

"Of course, I can, Vinny, it's the line and the distance, sorry!"

"Oh, okay! Listen I'd like two more of these cane sets from Nagaland. One for Chandigarh and the other I will sell at double the price, good idea don't you think? It'll pay for my transport unless Gurbir Chacha does the needful through the army. Oof! This set is looking so good. Hello, Ras? Hello! Hello!"

The mist suddenly swirled into the hall along with a gust of wind, dislodging a golf cap from the wooden hatstand.

I shifted uncomfortably on my feet not knowing how to respond to Vinny's chatter about cane sets from Nagaland. It was then that I heard a shot followed by several cracker-like bursts.

"Vinny, I'll call you back in the evening—bye—yes, yes, don't worry."

In a flash I was back at the window. Three figures were tumbling down the slope through the mist, carrying what seemed, from where I stood, like a long duffle bag. Out of the cottage a fourth figure emerged, carrying a small suitcase and walking quickly through the mist down to the stream, at the foot of the hillock. Just before he disappeared from sight, the slim, medium built figure in a maroon shirt looked back at the cottage once.

I ran back to the phone.

It was dead.

3

ON THE HILL opposite, a tall white house with windows like tired, hollow eyes rose above a cluster of small hill cottages, red roofed and innocent. Inside, a man moved away from a window. He put down his binoculars, lit a cigarette and offered one to his companion.

"There was a woman at the window. She saw everything. It wasn't the old lady."

"What? We've had it! I thought everyone was out of town. How could this happen? Wasn't it quite certain that there's nobody there? How is this possible?"

"Stop panicking, Ksan. Never panic. There's no problem that cannot be solved. I've had the phone line cut. The rest we will take care of."

Then he dialled a number.

4

I RUSHED TO THE kitchen. It was quiet, at peace, a picture of perfect domestic calm.

It was bathed in a soft light… the last of the day and the lace curtains were billowing gently in the breeze

Kmie U Flin had prepared tea for me. It was five o'clock and teatime in Shillong. On the pale blue traycloth with a sprinkling of pink and lilac flowers on four sides, were two cups, a matching milk jug, a sugar bowl and a teapot all in pale pink.

I stared at Kmie U Flin to see if there was any trace of panic or worry on her face but there was none. It seemed she had neither heard nor seen anything. Very quietly, as she always did, she said, "Pour yourself a cup of tea before it gets cold. Come, Kong Raseel enjoy your tea."

I continued to look at her, confused and wondering if the events of the past few minutes were but a figment of my imagination. There was Kmie U Flin shuffling around as she always did. She had been brought here many years ago as a young widow to serve as a live-in domestic help—this was normal practice in many well-to-do families. She had four, no three children, all proudly named after Hollywood stars by her husband, the late Bah Kwinton. So there was Errol Flynn Kharkongor, James Dean Kharkongor and the youngest, Sophialamon Kharkongor. The Khasi touch for Sophia was probably because she was a daughter, a 'khadduh', who would have been custodian of the family property and with whom the parents would have traditionally lived. Tragedy struck, however, and Sophia died of dysentery as a child and all her mother wanted to do was leave her village of Marbisu forever. Kharkongor is one of the noble clans of the Khasi Hills, this was also taken into account by the family when they asked her to move in.

"What are you staring at Kong Raseel? Is the tray-cloth stained?" Kmie U Flin stood in front of me with worried eyes, a plate of cucumber sandwiches in one hand and Mahari mixed cakes in the other. Delicious cakes. They used to be fifteen rupees a pound when I was in school long ago.

"No, the traycloth is not stained, Kmie U Flin." I started laughing. Obsession with cleanliness is an endearing Khasi trait. "Come, let's have tea, Kmie U Flin, here have this jam tart—yum!" I said, trying desperately to cling to normalcy.

Kmie U Flin had always been treated with respect because of her age and background. There was always a guarded pretence of equality with her by everyone in the family. No one disturbed the magnanimity and genuine affection, which the loyal domestic never abused. On her part she never forgot her place in one of the wealthiest families of these hills belonging to a clan that once ruled the hima of Mawsynram, the place which, not so long ago, had recorded rainfall even higher than Cherrapunjee.

"Kmie U Flin," I said as she settled down on a mula near me with her mug of tea, "do people around here carry guns?"

"Guns? Yes, yes the police and those CRPF men… wherever they are patrolling," she replied, biting into the jam tart, then she added, "militants too and naughty boys but not openly of course. That's what Robart tells me. I am so happy the traycloth is not stained. Is the tea all right?"

Kmie U Flin wasn't pretending, all she was worried about at that point was something going wrong with her perfectly laid out tea. Obviously Aunty Rosamon had schooled her well: tea should be consumed serenely, in the right place with the right conversation and the appropriate China cups and other accessories. Why should I spoil it all with my own neuroses, why destroy this idyll, I ruminated, as Kmie U Flin brought out a freshly baked plain cake from the oven.

Such an immense relief to be away from Delhi where even the hint of a blank look from me would have Renu Masi and Cousin Sonia rushing to the phone to speak with my psychiatrist, Minna Jaiswal. They would have termed my behaviour the 'latest development' in hushed tones. Minna Jaiswal came into my life three years ago and weaned me away from the deep depression I'd sunk into after the murder of my parents in Delhi by their domestic help. Now, it was so refreshing to be somewhere else, in a place where a blank look was simply associated with a stain on a traycloth.

I shivered as the mist swirled in through an open window.

"Kmie U Flin, please close the window."

"Yes, yes, mosquitoes will get in, that's the problem with summer."

"Kmie U Flin where is the PCO?"

"The what, Kong Raseel?"

"The telephone booth."

"Phone? It's in the hall. There's an extension here too. The cake...good?"

"The phone is dead. Yes, yes the cake is good. The phone is dead Kmie U Flin."

"Oh! That happens once in a while. It'll get fixed once Robart comes. He has a mobile. He'll call."

Robert Nongaren, Aibor's cousin who also worked for the family and who Kmie U Flin looked upon as a son.

"Where's Robert?"

"He has gone to buy some fruit, pineapples are excellent in this season and he's bringing some pork too. I will make doh iong for you. I know you like it—or would you prefer chicken? There's some in the fridge."

"Kmie U Flin tell me, who lives in the cottage in the orchard?"

"Sures and Rabi. I hope Robart doesn't forget my kwai and tympew."

Suresh and Ravi. I froze. The names clearly suggested that they were 'dkhars', outsiders, plainsmen but I still persisted with my questions, hoping against hope.

"Yes," Kmie U Flin replied cheerily. "Wonderful boys from Bihar. Our boys don't work half as hard as them. Always taking leave and in a day they take four, five breaks smoking their pipes or lying on their backs staring at the sky as if...."

"Kmie U Flin please could you call them. I want to talk to them. And there's nothing wrong with staring at the sky, it's the most divine experience... but please go and call Suresh and Ravi first." I could hear the panic in my words and feel the beginnings of that familiar throbbing in my head. I rushed to a window and took three, deep long breaths. I learnt that at a Yoga centre in Rishikesh.

"Kong Raseel, what is it that you would like? They are gardeners, they have nothing to do with the house. Robart will come soon and do something about the phone. Have your tea, another cup. You should always sip it calmly, only then will it be of any benefit. Nowadays..."

"Yes, yes Kmie U Flin nobody realizes all this nowadays, the right thoughts, the right conversation, the right surroundings even the right clothes during tea time. Come, come, let us go down to the gardener's cottage. I feel I need a short walk. I'll have more tea, with everything absolutely perfect the way Aunty Rosamon would have liked, later. Come."

There must have been a certain firmness in my voice and resolve in the way I stood up because she stopped, paused, did a turnaround and walked out into the mist without saying a word. I followed her rather guiltily—I had never been so curt with her before. I was relieved when I heard her starting to hum softly, an easy familiar tune that floated through the air like a wandering cloud. I watched her digging her hand into the ubiquitous cloth bag that hung from a strap on her left shoulder across her bosom down to her right hip, for some kwai. My throat knotted and my eyes smarted. It took me back thirty years—mom, dad, lambent sunshine and laughing Khasi maids, Jenny, Christina and little Annie, Jenny's daughter.

5

"WHY DIDN'T YOU tell us that there was a house guest?" the man slurred into the phone, while his companion listened intently.

"She wasn't expected so soon. Apparently, Kong Aila was not sure whether her guest was coming or not..." the man replied and was cut short.

"How close is she to the family, Ksan?"

"Very close, Strong, very close."

"Shit! Let us clear our heads before we tell the Boss. I have to work it out anyway."

Then both of them sank into the sofas and grabbed some much-needed sleep.

6

KMIE U FLIN stood on her toes, tall enough for her voice to travel over the hedge of azaleas that stretched along the road above the orchard.

"Sures, ko Sures, Rabi, ko Rabi" she called out through the failing light as a light drizzle suddenly fell from the sky. My teeth chattered and I took deep breaths as I tried to herd all the negative feelings into a distant corner of my mind. I echoed Kmie U Flin.

"Sures ko Sures, Rabi ko Rabi."

We were greeted by a deep silence. It was so quiet, as quiet as the beginning of Time. I wrapped my arms around myself trying to control my heart which was beating fast, like a bird in panic. I felt very scared. I could feel the fear creeping in. "Where are these boys? They don't normally go out on weekdays. Even on Sundays they go out only during the day. I will tell Robart to give them a good lecture. This is no way to behave. Anyway there's nothing to worry about."

Even as she said it I knew Kmie U Flin, sensing my fear, was just trying to reassure me. "Should I…?" but before I could articulate what I wanted to, there was a blackout and the lights went off. As we stumbled through the dark I realized to my horror that, besides the three local boys, I had seen only one other boy leaving the cottage.

"Come Kong Raseel, we will go and have some tea," she spoke loudly as if darkness made men deaf but more to convince herself that all was well.

As we trudged back my head sat like an enormous boulder on my shoulders, solemn, unmoving. Beneath it I could feel myself crumbling. Is this all a dream? Maybe Minna Jaiswal was right. I exaggerated events just to reassure myself that worse things could happen than knowing your parents were murdered, butchered by a man they trusted. At a lunch at the Delhi Gymkhana Club when Minna and cousin Vinny and I suddenly erupted into a heated discussion on trust, I remembered commenting that trusting was a criminal act because of the gigantic responsibility it placed on the person you trust. Anything that weighed down a human being was a crime worse than all the crimes ever enumerated. That evening I was given a new strip of medicines.

"Come, Kong Raseel" Kmie U Flin was saying, "I will serve pure, light Darjeeling with some lemon. It's very refreshing. Oh! Look, there's Robart."

The headlights of a car pierced the darkness that was slowly descending. The car purred to a halt at the porch and Robert tumbled out carrying two loaded bags of shopping.

"Robart, the lights have gone off, the phone is dead and Sures and Rabi are not in their rooms," Kmie U Flin rattled off the complaints whilst offering to help with the bags.

I thought I sensed a tense anger in Robert but I wasn't sure for his reply was casual and carefree.

"Oh! Don't worry. They must be watching a film on TV. They are young boys, they may have gone out to visit their cousins who are employed not far from here."

"Where? I've never heard of these cousins, Robart," Kmie U Flin interjected, sounding a little piqued.

"You have never heard of so many things Meisan, come let us go in. This rain is treacherous. It usually comes when you least expect it. You have yet to experience it this time,

Kong but you will. you will! We'll get wet and yet not feel cold and tomorrow we'll be in bed with fever," said Robert, calm and collected, holding Kmie U Flin by her shoulders.

"Robert, have you had tea?" I asked.

"Yes, Kong Raseel .... At Bah Ellis'."

"He means Kong Bet's, this rogue," said Kmie U Flin, smiling, snuggling up to Robert like a fond parent. "There is no harm in admiring beauty but remember she is married, Robart."

"All right, all right Meisan. Bah Ellis was still at work but the beautiful Kong Bet didn't serve me tea either, her mother did. On top of that she forgot to put in sugar, she added too much milk and I could do nothing about it. But, yes, she served me crisp pyllon shroin and I have brought some for Kong Raseel to have with her morning tea."

"Thank you so much Robert..."

"Now we will all have ..."

"No, Kmie U Flin no more tea. We will all have wine. Ok, folks I know it's not done normally, but I have come from far, far away after a long, time so let's have a party! Bah Aibor and Kong Aila will understand. Don't worry I will explain it to them. Promise! I really want to chat and relax, folks!" I tried to sound casual and cheerful butI was apprehensive. After all one didn't spend evenings drinking with one's staff. I prayed that the evening would flow as it should and wouldn't degenerate into stilted conversation and unbridgeable gaps.

Robert picked up the local paper and started reading it. Kmie U Flin pulled back her shoulders, put up her little nose and very proudly said to me, "Kong Aila does give me brandy when it gets very cold, it really helps. Unfortunately I now have this sugar disease so she stopped giving it to me except once in a while. Robart bring your glass and you can have it in your room. I will have mine before going to bed, in my room...."

"No, no no," I interrupted, amused and yet horrified by her plan. "We will not have wine separately. We will sit together wherever you all feel comfortable and enjoy it together. I want to chat, yes, I just want to chat."

Two pairs of eyes stared back at me. One pair was filled with surprise and affection, the other with suspicion.

7

"THE WOMAN FROM Delhi, damn her, went to the cottage to find out if those boys were there."

"Shit!"

"I believe nobody in the house knew about this woman's arrival."

"How can that be?"

"She apparently said she wanted to give Aibor and Aila a surprise when they return."

"Hah! Surprise!"

"She's on some nostalgic trip. She grew up here, studied with Kong Aila. They are good friends."

"Shut UP!" shouted Strong. "Gossiping like a woman. Let's focus on the problem—this woman saw everything."

"I am as worried, Strong."

"Nothing to worry about. I have a remedy, as always."

"I don't like the look in your eyes, she could be some VIP's wife, daughter, sister and..."

"I am not thinking what you are thinking dumbo," Strong growled and he bared his teeth in a sinister grin.

8

I KNEW I WAS doing everything wrong. Immediately after I heard the gunshot and realized that the phone was dead, I should have run up the hill, out of the gate, up the second slope and traversed the country lane to reach the market and the nearest PCO. I should have called the Police, the other school friends in town, Aila's father and brothers. They could have contacted Aibor who was, along with Aila, sightseeing in China, viewing the only 'wonder of the world' that they hadn't seen, the Great Wall.

On that August evening, however, everything seemed to alternate between nightmare and dream. And with those around me so calm, casual and dismissive, my reaction seemed totally out of character.

I went over the scene again and again, the attire of the men, their build and features, their body language. I did the same with the lone boy who had fled the scene, after what I thought were gunshots. The way he walked away almost in slow motion.

I guess I felt foolish talking about all of this because I simply wasn't sure. For quite a while after my parents' murder I was prone to hallucinations. Minna confirmed it. It was the scariest period of my life. I certainly didn't want a relapse. If I didn't speak about something, I could sit on it. But giving words to the thought somehow gave it flesh and blood.

And then, there didn't seem to be a crisis here at all. Honestly, that was what I told myself as I sat in that green, tin roofed hill bungalow with the mist all around, lace curtains billowing in the wind, quiet everywhere.

9

IN THE HOTEL room of an up-market locality the men sat sipping Peter Scot. There was a third person with Strong and Ksan and three other boys in jeans and jackets.

"Anyway," he said, adjusting his elegant tie around his slender neck that held a refined face with Mongolian features. "What did the woman see? Three men carrying a bag and another one leaving with a suitcase? That's all. What's so abnormal? They have all disappeared due to the robbery. That's it. As for the gunshots, that Marwari family was bursting crackers all day. That one shot couldn't have been that loud—what did you use?" he addressed a young, leather jacketed man, puffing at his India Kings imperiously.

The boy shuffled uncomfortably and answered, "An AK 47".

"Hmn... anyway, as Bah Strong said we should not panic. All that is expected of you all is absolute loyalty.

We think, we plan, we tell you what to do. Ksan, did you find out more details about this woman?"

"No. She seems harmless enough, innocent but snoopy and also strange. She hasn't told anyone, not even those two at home."

"Who's the cop investigating this case?"

"We don't know yet."

"You don't know yet? It's almost five hours now and you don't know yet? Where's my mobile? You young ones may leave now. See that tonight's plan doesn't turn out to be another free movie show."

Taking a huge gulp from his glass he punched furiously at the numbers of his mobile.

The three boys walked out of the room to rejoin their companions in the waiting car outside, a common and innocent looking old, green Gypsy.

10

BY THE TIME Robert came up from his room, positioned at one end of the main staff quarters, I was ready with the wine and banana chips brought from a corner shop in Delhi.

Robert had spruced up and looked good. I had always found him handsome. He was, after all, not only Aibor's second or third cousin but also of mixed parentage. His father was a Sindhi businessman, whose Sindhi wife wisely overlooked her husband's local liaison, for the gains in this alien territory were many and lucrative. Needless to say, he moved on from his Khasi wife as soon as he was established. He provided for her, bought her a three bedroom house with a garden in Malki. Actually she had begun to get used to him, to love him, in fact, but she was far too proud to tell her husband to stay, leave alone telling him to think of maintenance. She had too much self-respect to confront him about his betrayal. He hadn't told her he was a married man.

She didn't even know he had a wife tucked away in Bombay. So she simply pushed Sunil Sindhwani out of her life forever. Later she married a Khasi and had two children before he, too, moved on.

Robert sat on the mula a little away from the fire. "It's warm," he said, and it was, but Kmie U Flin had lit the fire just for my sake. She remembered that I enjoyed sitting near it and it always made me feel wonderful. She had kept a chair for me, a perfectly crafted cane chair with a soft cushion in a satin cover. I pushed it gently away saying, "Please Kmie U Flin just this once" and dragged a mula right next to them before anyone could protest. Then I turned to Robert.

"Robert, now tell me what all has been happening with you, we have thirty years to catch up on.... Oh! Well ... maybe let's just hear some stories, stories you tell your children like the ones we used to hear as kids, folk tales. Remember Sier Lapalang? I used to love that story. I believe Lord Mountbatten wanted the folk song to be sung at his funeral. Kmie U Flin was so good with all that but she's busy. Let's just talk, about anything you feel like."

Kmie U Flin, who had taken her glass to the kitchen, peeped in and acknowledged my remembering with the sweetest of smiles. That gesture put me at ease. I needed so much to be reassured.

"Stories?" Robert laughed a little too loud, startling me. "Firstly my children all live with their mother. She left me and remarried. Even when we were all together where was the time for stories? It was TV and more TV, once their homework was done."

"What did they watch Robert?"

"Sports, cartoons, serials but most of all Hindi films."

"Hindi films?"

"Yes, see my kids didn't go to an English medium school so it's not AXN, Star World, and all that. It's Hindi films and songs."

"Strange isn't it Robert that there's all this hype about outsiders, plainsmen? I would imagine that people here would not accept anything from the mainland, 'India' as they call it."

"Kong Raseel nobody considers Amitabh Bacchan, Shahrukh Khan, Aishwarya Rai and Preity Zinta dkhars. They are from the skies, the stars. Hah! The stars..." he shouted and took a big swig from his glass.

"How about asking them to come here and talk about, say, national unity and all that, about the true feelings of the mainlanders about how we are one people, one country?"

"The true feelings Kong? Hah! We all know what the true feelings are. Let's face it, the dkhars will always look down on us tribals."

"Robert, in India everyone looks down on everyone, The Brahmins turn up their noses on the Kshatriyas, the Kshatriyas look down on the Kayasths, the Kayasths on the Vaishyas and it just goes on. My parents were both Sikhs but my mother had to rebel when she married my father because he wasn't a Jat Sikh. One has to be confident of one's worth as a human being and just believe, believe in a world where the mind is without fear and the head is held high. Remember Tagore?"

Robert looked down at his toes. My eyes wandered away to the window. On the opposite hill something was burning, the flames leaping up almost playfully as if it was a game. But I knew it wasn't.

11

THE WOMAN WATCHED the fire slowly die into gray dust and the monsoon wind sweeping it all away. She chewed her kwai noisily, as she lay sprawled across a coarsely carved divan.

The phone rang.

"Is it over?" the man at the other end asked.

"Yes, you can come back whenever you wish."

"Did you inform the police, the rangbah shnong, the Press and the neighbours?"

"Yes, yes, they were all here. Bah Heh is handling them like a good son. My absence is overlooked because of my blood pressure and gout."

"Ok. What's for dinner?"

"Pork in boiled cabbage, fried fish..."

"Good, I'll start off after an hour or so. If anyone else rings up to inquire, please sound suitably agitated. Remember I am in Ron's farm out of reach by telephone and I left my mobile behind."

"I know, I know. And now that our car is burnt to cinders when do we get a new car?"

But the man had hung up.

12

KMIE U FLIN stood rooted by the window, speechless. Robert kept sipping his wine calmly as though nothing was happening. When I could bear it no longer I asked.

"What's happening? What are they burning?"

"A minister's car."

"Why?"

"There's an agitation against the government about quotas for education and jobs. The Garos don't deserve 40 per cent, the vacancies are never filled, they go waste, and we are more deserving."

"More?"

"Yes, Khasis and Jaintias 60 per cent and Garos 30 per cent... and the rest 10 per cent. It's reasonable."

"Yes?"

"Kong, please relax. It's all very complicated so don't try to understand."

"Don't listen to him! Robart stop it. It must be an accident. Why should they burn Bah Jus' car. He's a good man, a good MLA. He's not the Chief Minister."

"He's part of the cesspool...and by the way Meisan he's trying very hard to become the Chief Minister. How would you know? For forty odd years you have been closeted here in the lap of luxury, how would you know what is happening beyond these four walls?"

Kmie U Flin gasped, her hands flew to her mouth and her frail body sank into my chair as she began to sob. I held her close, as my eyes captured the sight of billowing smoke and my ears caught the sound of buckets of water being thrown, like waves on a moonlit shore.

Against it all was silhouetted the chiselled face of Robert Nongrum—head held high, mouth calm, eyes resolute.

"Let's have dinner Kmie U Flin. Yes, you go and heat it, thank you."

When she had disappeared into the kitchen, I went and sat next to Robert.

"Robert, I know that saying 'why don't people just talk things out' is easy, but this is no solution. It never has been."

"How can there be a solution when nobody is articulating the problem? Some don't even know it."

"But you said it's about seats and jobs."

"That's what's floating on top. The dkhars are all usurping our jobs—get them out, they are stealing our women—kill them, the Garos are letting the seats go waste, they could never fill the 40 per cent so let's protest."

"Yeah, so that's it."

"No. That is not it. Over the years all that has increased and multiplied are the number of protestors! That is the only progress made. They come from the villages where there is no development, because the MLA couldn't care less. They come here and realize that it isn't all that easy, well at least for most of them—so they turn to all sorts of crime or they simply drink, drug and sell themselves...in different ways. Eventually they join the new Employment Exchange."

"Oh! Really?"

"Yes, don't you know? The work is very easy, the pay excellent. Extort, burn, kill, ask no questions. 'If you've got guts, here's the gun, follow our orders and collect your paycheck.' That is it, Kong Raseel."

"Robert, for God's sake, what are you saying?"

"I am telling you the truth. We talk so lightly of truth... truth is not what each one thinks is the truth. That is not correct, Kong. What we flaunt as the truth is only a reflection of our fallible minds. Go a little deeper and then one gets to see the larger picture, the deeper truth, the reality. That is when one faces the only truth, deep down there it stares you in the face like a demon, unmoving."

"What is the demon saying, Robert? Does it have a voice?"

"Sure it has. It speaks through the horrors that erupt all the time—but no one listens. Everyone hears but no one listens. Look Kong Raseel, let me not beat about the bush... the men here are in a terrible state. We are sad, we are desperate and all these terrible emotions stem from that. We own not a patch of land, not a penny, nothing. Even our children belong to their mothers. If we get a government job—fine. If not—then what? Rot... Yes, we are doing something now. We are fighting for equitable distribution of wealth and registration of marriages but till all this comes through most of us just float around like scum in a stagnant well. Yeah, that's it. That's the truth!"

Tears welled up in his eyes which were red as live coals. He was holding the stem of the wine glass so tightly that it broke and drops of blood stained his hands, and fell on the Tibetan rug on the floor.

I touched his shoulder. Framed against the door opposite was Kmie U Flin.

"What is he doing? What is he talking about? He has never talked like this before. Robart what has happened, son? You've never talked like this before! Why are you complaining so much? My child, you are whining like a school boy. Robart this is not you. Stop drinking. Throw away that drink!"

"I won't Meisan. I will drink and I will whine and complain... and drink some more and whine and complain. I need to do it. Why haven't I done it before? You are asking me, Meisan?"

I noticed the anger in his eyes. I felt the need to step in.

"No, he couldn't have talked about this earlier because as he said nobody listens. Oh! Kmie U Flin don't look so sad."

I started to cry. The tears flowed like the bursting of a dam. And I let them. It was exactly what I needed. I had never felt so scared.

13

"WHILE HER CAR was burning Bah Jus' wife apparently didn't show enough fear... or panic."

"What do you expect? She is beautiful but a bloody fool. Anyway no one suspected anything. There was plenty of commotion."

"Yeah. As long as this CM goes and Bah Jus' comes in he may be able to do something about the quotas."

"Stop it Ksan. Don't try to pretend to me. Who cares about all that as long as we get our way?"

"Don't be so angry, Strong. What way, anyway?"

"Actually I don't know, Ksan."

14

"KMIE U FLIN, What about Suresh and Ravi?" I asked.

"Robart?"

"Their lights are off. They must be asleep. Kong Raseel, Meisan is telling you about her cousin, Bah Hekstar. Yes, he did marry the youngest daughter of the family. Yes, he is highly respected: yes, he is loved, yes, he's happy. You know why? Because he moved in as a rich man. A successful smuggler—as a young man he turned to trade and became respectable and now his children are all professionals. It all comes down to economics. But how many people can be successful smugglers and bootleggers? It's as difficult as getting a government job! You want to start something on your own, where's the money? We can't even approach the bank because there's no one to stand guarantee for us. You tell your sisters and they pretend ignorance, some offer their sympathies. You turn to your parents and they give you a lecture on customs and the laws of inheritance in a matrilineal society. So you go to your room and drink yourself to sleep. If you are married you go to a bed, to a woman who really doesn't need you after a while."

"Robart..."

"The men here are... well see first they were bewildered and wondered what was happening. So they pinpointed the problem, an easy, comfortable explanation to their...what did I say? Yeah, bewilderment. They worked out this great big solution and we got a state of our own. Still things were going wrong so they zeroed on all the outsiders 'because they are stealing our jobs'. Except for those who had the money to pay, the rest had their houses burnt, their bodies battered. Many fled, some clung on, the Bengalis, Nepalis, Biharis and, of course, wealthy Marwaris, Sindhis, Sikhs. They stayed but they lived according to the new rules. Everyone knows his place. Yet things are still going wrong. So now it's become the Garos. These are all punching bags. Out of sheer frustration we punch, we shoot, we... kill. I feel so, I think this is the main cause of all this goddamned frustration and I think I am right. Every Khasi man feels so faltu, so completely and utterly helpless."

"Robart, maternal uncles and brothers are highly respected in every Khasi home. Without their knowledge and permission no important decision is ever made."

"That was long ago Meisan, before the priests replaced them. Who asks a Mama for permission and all that stuff nowadays? They ask the priest. Especially in homes like ours Meisan, homes of converts. The children don't see their Mamas for months and months. Who needs them unless they are 'somebody'? Hah! So tell me, Kong, how can we cling to the matrilineal system when it has been so badly eroded? It has to be amended. It has to be refashioned in keeping with the times. These days land translates into money and money into Ultimate Bliss and we men are entitled to nothing… nothing."

Kmie U Flin just stared at Robert, speechless, unbelieving. I put my arm around her and gently stroked her head till she calmed down and started to cry.

I could feel the shock and bewilderment with every sob of hers as despair filled my heart on that warm August evening in a faraway hill town.

15

"HOW MANY?"

"Five government cars—two jeeps, three Ambassadors and a private car."

"Why a private car?"

"Bah Jus' car. Just to...you know! Have you already hit the bottle or what? Don't you remember? No one should guess he is with the Boss. After all he is an MLA and a member of the party. Now he'll able to function freely and his ministers will do the rest."

"His ministers?"

"Yes, he's bought two of them. They will do the needful. That is what the Boss said."

"And..."

"And Strong, please don't drink too much when there is work to be done."

"And?"

"Strict instructions have been issued that we must show that this agitation is not ethnic or communal, it is simply anti-government. That's very important. I don't have to elaborate."

"I know, I know."

16

BY THE TIME I woke up the sun was high and strong, slanting into my room through the east-facing window fronted by pots of geraniums. There were loud, desperate knocks on my door. As I opened it Titi, the daily help, flew into my room almost dropping the morning tea-tray. She was shaking.

"Kong, Kong! Sures and Rabi have disappeared!"

"Why didn't you wake me up earlier?"

"Bah Robart said you need rest. Oh! Kong the police have come and so many others…"

I wrapped my arms tightly around myself. The nightmare began to surface again. I swallowed a Valium and munching two Marie biscuits, poured myself a cup of tea. Titi sat on the mat on the floor and started to cry. I kept pacing the room, not knowing what to do next. There was no escaping the truth now. I watched the sunbeams dancing on my quilt and my mind went blank.

"There's blood on the walls..."

"Where?"

"In the gardener's cottage, Kong. What is happening? I am feeling so scared. Oh! Kong!" and suddenly, she rushed towards me and clung to my legs like a leech. I was as scared as Titi and unhinged by this unusual show of emotion, so unlike a Khasi. I put my hand on her head. I felt completely marooned in an island of deep sadness and guilt.

The policeman was scribbling furiously in his note-book, when I went down. A chair had been brought out for him. He sat in the morning sun in the slightly overgrown lawn in his starched uniform and mirror-shine shoes. A little way away in a separate group—distinctly different in every way—sat the rangbah shnong, the local headman and a few neighbours and well-wishers. Aibor's two brothers arrived in their shining Santros and I sighed with immense relief when I saw Aila's father, Uncle Rangshan, arriving in his superbly preserved Ambassador. I ran into his arms and hugged him tight. He had come alone. When Aunty Rosamon died he remarried and moved to his second wife's house. Aunty Binola was a childless widow. Everyone was relieved because Uncle Rangshan was an extremely attractive man and had a legion of admirers, most of them not so suitable.

The cop was questioning Robert.

"Around 8 am, I came up to clean the cars. Suresh normally helps me with that. I was surprised when he was not here. So I called out to him and Ravi. When nobody responded I went down to the cottage. "

"Before that you had no inkling of their absence? You are all in the same compound, Robert."

"No, no, I knew nothing till I went down to the cottage this morning and realized the boys were missing and Ravi's belongings all gone. They had few belongings but I could recognize Suresh's pants and shirts and his suitcase in the room." Robert answered without a moment's hesitation.

My heart stopped as I studied my neglected toes that peeked out of my Marie Claire sandals. Robert was lying. He had put me in a fix. What was I supposed to do? I would go completely mad if I had to bottle up yesterday's events.

"Well," hummed the cop, "it seems like a serious case of robbery. One of them is the robber and the other the victim. Tch! Tch! The law and order situation in the state is terrible… I believe the victim had a whole year's salary with him, Robert."

"Yes, he didn't go on leave so all that money must have been in the suitcase which is now missing."

Kmie U Flin sidled up to me and, squeezing my hand, whispered, "Don't worry. I don't know why he said what he said but I am not letting anyone cast aspersions on Rabi and Sures just like that," and tidying up her hair and jainkyrshah she walked towards the cop. Uncle Rangshan was desperately trying to contact Aibor through a friend's son who worked in a hotel in Shanghai.

"Look Bah," Kmie U Flin said, "I am quite sure that nobody robbed and nobody killed. NOT my boys. They loved each other like brothers. They worked together, stayed together, ate, drank and laughed together. They are from the same village!"

"Look Kong. Crime is not as simple as all that, you know. Money is always a huge temptation. I deal with this every day. Understand?"

Kmie U Flin glared at him but was rendered speechless. She had not met a cop before, ever. I decided to step in. For some reason the cop looked up and rose to his full height of five feet four inches and gave a small, brisk bow.

"Yes Ma'am. You are?"

"I am Raseel Singh. I am a childhood friend of Aila's. We were here in Loreto together. I came here a few days ago from Delhi." I shook his hand. Nice handshake, neither too hard nor spongy.

"I see, I see" he said, chirpily, and continued to stand. "How do you like the weather? Not raining too much this year. Climate changes you know all over... all over."

"I am used to it."

"Yes, yes. How long are you staying?"

I found his question not only rude but disturbing—more disturbing than rude actually.

"Officer, Kmie U Flin is absolutely correct. I, too, do not think it's a simple case of robbery. I also think both the Bihari boys are innocent. The one who has disappeared is not the perpetrator."

"The what?"

"The culprit."

"Really?" his eyes narrowed and he looked at me deep and hard. "You have been here only three days...five days ok, how can you be so sure about all this?"

"Last evening, just before dusk I saw one of the boys leaving the cottage with his belongings, well, a suitcase..."

"He was running?"

"No, he was walking away with a suitcase in his hand and he looked back at the cottage once and then carried on down the slope. He was not running. He didn't seem like a man on the run."

"I see, I see. How do you know that he was carrying his belongings?"

"OK, I don't know what he was carrying, Well, I am as ignorant as you are." I smiled at him and he, too flashed back his small, pearly white, almost womanly teeth. I continued undeterred, "Before that three men came to the cottage, one went inside and two stood around in the verandah. One of the men in the verandah had leucoderma."

I was hoping that would have the effect of a Hiroshima bomb but I was wrong. He simply nodded and wrote it down in his notebook and thanked me as if all I had done was to give him information on the latest weather condition... not even an earthquake. I think I stared at him with my mouth wide open. That was how I found myself when someone touched my shoulder. We walked away. Inside I was screaming, "Are we here to investigate a crime or nail an innocent boy?"

We walked away, Uncle Rangshan and I, to the comforting shade of the old chestnut tree and I took three deep breaths chanting, "Shanti Shanti Shanti."

Uncle Rangshan held me, saying, "Yes, say your prayers."

"Uncle, I am sure it's not the Bihari boy."

"Raseel, Robert is saying he tried his best to keep you out of it. I didn't hear what you told the police officer but ..."

"Uncle, I have to tell the cop what I saw, what I think. This has nothing to do with Robert."

What on earth had I got myself into? Is this the summer of madness that Aila and I had planned over telephonic giggles? Innocent plans to relive our childhood strolls through pine scented forests and along quiet lakes full of secrets, to rest our eyes on emerald hills that roll on and on in the distance to touch a sapphire sky. Maybe we focused too much on the word 'madness' and now that was exactly what was happening.

17

"THE COP HAS left," said the man switching off his mobile, the man was on the opposite hill, in the tall, white house with windows like tired eyes.

His companion, unmoved, kept looking out of the window, puffing furiously. Finally he spoke,

"Did she…?"

"Yes, she did. She said she saw three guys in the cottage. First they left and the dkhar left a little later. One dkhar. She also said one of the three guys had leucoderma."

"Get Ribok on the line. He has to leave immediately. It will be difficult in this weather but he will have to manage."

"He will. Kong Rivulet returned a few days ago. She said it was tough especially because of the leeches but she…."

"Still managed and brought a lot of 'maal'. I admire that woman. I hope she has brought some jackets."

"Is that all you want?"

"Yeah, at this moment. Did you get Ribok?"

The youngest of the three, in a peak cap and matching sneakers, nodded and said, "But he says he has fever…"

"Give me the phone. Ribok? Yeah, yeah just carry some paracetemol and run. Once you cross the border you will be well looked after."

18

I FELT RELIEVED AND completely exhausted after the cop left. The sun suddenly disappeared and clouds gathered in the sky. For a long time I didn't speak to Uncle Rangshan who sat quietly by my side. Aila's brothers, and several of her relatives and friends were engrossed in whispered discussions.

A strong smell of rain wafted into the room and the whispers stopped. Everyone sat hunched and silent like old monks in prayer, decoding the messages of the turbulent sky. In the distance the thunder rumbled and flashes of light, sharp. swift, sword-like lit up the sky while the rain poured steadily, regally, undeterred.

"Raseel, you should have called me up immediately when you saw those boys."

"I didn't think there was anything unusual Uncle," I lied.

"I suppose so … but I wish you had mentioned it to Kmie U Flin or even Robert."

I kept quiet.

How much can one lie? Uncle Rangshan looked so concerned. I knew he was as worried for me as he was for Aila and Aibor. I put my head on his shoulder and closed my eyes.

19

IN A ROOM inside the tall house the phone rang.

All at once the atmosphere changed, the tension was palpable. Another day had passed. It was the midnight of the day after. Strong and Ksan looked fatigued but charged.

"I know there was no audience this time," he said gruffly into the phone. "How many houses? OK, hmn… come right away. No, just walk, walk through the locality lanes, and pretend you are drunk. Two of you can do that. Talk about a Hindi film, hum a tune. That will throw the CRPF guys totally off scent. Come."

"Why tonight? Strong, they could have…"

"No, no. I want them to report eye to eye. They should always report this way. Just hearing is not enough. I want to see these boys, their body language, their tone, their eyes.

They have to see ME. I have to make them burn inside like we used to… Like WE used to."

Strong grunted and pulling the bottle of whiskey out of the cabinet poured a drink for himself.

"It's a bit early isn't it?"

"What's early and what's late? I am so tired, I am so goddamned tired."

"That's exactly what I am saying, why call them tonight?"

"I am so tired of it all Ksan. Not of just this moment but I am tired of it all, ALL of this SHIT," he shouted. "Where is all this going to lead? We are just following the Boss' orders. It's been going on for so long."

"He thinks, plans, orders and…"

"And we follow, right? Yet does that scum care? Will all this really bring the government to the table? Does the government care? Does Delhi care? Does anyone care? Or are we being used, just simply being used for the Boss' gains? He is using us, Ksan. He is using these kids too."

"Yes…"

"Yes and look at us now… mere castrated bulls."

"Shut up, Strong."

"I won't." And pouring another drink he sipped, slurped. His eyes were closed; his hands were clenched as his heart burnt inside.

"Strong, go home and just relax for a while."

"Home? Hah! That hell, that is where all the trouble starts. Yesterday I told my wife that her mother was a fat sow and you know what she did? She walked off in a huff in the middle of the night and went and slept in that very sow's room, in her bed!"

"Well, I don't think it was right of you to call your kiaw a fat sow."

"Oh no? Oh yes, Ksan, YES! That old hag had the guts to tell me to throw away some orange peels!"

"So what? She's an elder."

"Don't butt in, listen. That bastard, Ken, my youngest sister-in-law's husband was the culprit. He was sitting on the steps, peeling orange after orange and throwing the peel around. He was sitting there eating oranges, spitting the seeds from his filthy mouth—couldn't care less, just like that, and I am supposed to..."

"Strong, that's bad."

"Yes and you also know why I am subjected to such treatment. I am not the khadduh's husband, I am not a government officer like that bloody slop, I can't move my wife and kids out from the family home, so this is what I get. THIS is what I GET."

"Just move out, Strong. If your wife can't stand by you, just move out."

"And go—where?"

"To your mother's house."

"Think first and then speak, Ksan. Think and then speak. Mei also has my youngest sister with her and there's her husband too…he's a cop but he's been kind though"

"Batriti is a good girl. She won't let her brother down."

"I am not so sure. Anyway, where do we go tonight once the kids are gone? How about that girl from Lummawbah? She seemed pretty keen huh?"

"Which one?"

"Well, the one I thought looked like Michelle Yeoh."

20

Two of Aila's aunts and their daughters moved in that same evening. Aila's brother too, with two other men who worked for him. Kmie U Flin buzzed around the house to make them comfortable. She readied the rooms and with the help of Titi, and a maid who worked for one of the aunts, whipped up a delicious dinner. Lunch had been brought from outside by one of the relatives. In between every now and again, she would sob, remembering the two missing boys. Everyone was upset that a crime had been committed in such a respectable house. Only Kmie U Flin was upset because Suresh and Ravi had disappeared.

That made two of us, just two of us.

21

"For your sister's sake, don't go around messing up your life. For the sake of your kids too."

Don't mention them Ksan. Don't. Shit I'm so fucking mad!"

"Stop it Strong!"

But it was too late. Strong had whipped out a penknife and slashed it across his palm.

"I want to erase these lines. This awful fate!"

"Strong..."

The blood started to drip. Ksan had never seen such bitterness, such sadness in his childhood friend. He started to shiver, feeling as if the entire universe was crumbling around him like old, worm-eaten walls.

Just then the there was a knock at the door. Three boys entered. They saw the blood; they said nothing.

"Sit down, tell us," Ksan whispered.

"How many houses?"

"Three."

"Did that khar suh nep flee? I mean was it done as it should have been done?"

"Yes. As soon as we started on him, his neighbour..."

"Kong Deng..."

"Yes, she came out and did her bit, she saved him as planned."

"That's good. He is a Mussulman, that community..."

"Yes we understand like...Bah Ribok...is...is..."

"On his way to the khar suh nep's country. Yes, that's the deal kids."

"Ok, you may all leave now. We'll let you know." Ksan said.

"Thanks boys. Well done!" Strong slurred and slumped back on the sofa.

The phone rang. Strong stretched his arm and picked it up.

"No," he said. "We have to stop the cops from going to Bihar. If they catch that fellow Rabi, we'll be in trouble. He left for Gorakhpur didn't he?"

22

NEXT MORNING I woke early and switched on Radio Shillong. I lay in bed for a while listening to the melodious Khasi songs sung by the beautiful Kong Helen Giri. The music transported me to a faraway land where Man and Nature merged in perfect melody. I didn't hear Titi coming in. She put down the tea tray and told me that Rabi had been caught and had confessed to the crime. She was hysterical. Her eyes were large pools of fear, her face ashen. She thrust the newspaper at me. My head spun as I read, "The murder of the Bihari employee of a private residence in Lawbah colony has been solved with the arrest of the victim's cousin, Ravi Rai, who has confessed to the crime, police sources confirmed today. The body of the victim has yet to be traced but the police are confident that the crime will be solved expediently after this breakthrough."

The newspaper slid to the floor as I stared at the rain pouring down from a gray impassive sky. It beat angrily on the tin roof that covered our large hill bungalow, and its residents who had so rudely been roused from their peaceful existence by a hitherto unknown and unimaginable incident. The rain continued its drumming on the tin roof. At least Nature commiserated with me and I felt somewhat at peace as my tea lay in front of me in a cane tray made in Tripura. I closed my eyes and imagined that my weary head rested on the shoulder of the mountain slope framed by my window. 'I live not in myself but I become/Portion of that around me; and to me/High mountains are a feeling.' I felt the tears stinging my eyes and I slipped into a second sleep, lulled by the words of an almost forgotten poem. When I woke up the skies had cleared, so typically Shillong. It was noon.

"Robert, I'd like to go for a drive."

"Where, Kong?"

"Anywhere."

"Why don't you visit someone? You will feel better. Kong Aila and Bah Aibor are probably arriving day after tomorrow."

"Let us go to town and beyond towards Nongthymmai. I will visit Sngithiang. You remember, no?"

"Yes, but they no longer stay there. They are now on the road behind the Raj Bhavan on the way to Golf Links. Her father is a Minister."

"Really, so let us go there. It is even closer."

Sngithiang—Sweet Sun—was in school with Aila and myself. She did her graduation from Shillong and also married her childhood boyfriend, Paul. She produced four kids and was happily married for twelve or thirteen years until his drinking started to upset her and she began to suffer from depression. Paul did not die of cirrhosis as many did in Shillong but one Sunday afternoon he slipped down Sngithiang's polished stairway and broke his neck. Aila told me that for many months Sngi (Nini) was inconsolable. She blamed her anti-depressant drugs for preventing her from waiting for her husband's lunch at 4pm "after all it was Sunday". She blamed Jackie Chan for keeping her children glued to the TV instead of escorting their inebriated father to the toilet, her parents for sleeping after lunch like plainsmen and her servants for going to church. I was very sad and shaken at the news of his death. Nini was one friend who used to extol the virtues of marriage: the exquisite feeling of complete fulfilment when she bathed, powdered and dressed each child, laid out their meals and watched them eat while she fed the youngest one, the joy of taking them out for drives and watching them play amidst the pines near Shillong Peak while she and Paul held hands, totally content. Alcoholism was a genetic problem in Paul's family or so it seemed. All his three maternal uncles died of excessive drinking.

As the car climbed up the slope, out of the wrought iron gate onto the main road, I felt my body loosening up. I leaned back and relaxed and told Robert to play an Elvis Presley cassette, softly. I let my eyes feast on all the sights that they could take in: houses with pots of geraniums blooming along with gerberas, daisies, pansies and orchids, their hues and shades dancing in the late morning sun. Was the day before yesterday a dream?

The Sanskrit name Meghalaya 'the Abode of the Clouds' was suggested by the linguist, Dr Suniti Kumar Chatterjee, who was doing a study in these hills between 1926 and 1932. Dr Chatterjee was apparently overwhelmed by the masses and masses of clouds that hung from the sky for days on end. The suggestion was taken up in 1971 when the Khasis, Jaintias and Garos separated from Assam and attained statehood and Shillong become the capital. By then I was in faraway Delhi but I joined the celebrations at an IAS officer's apartment in RK Puram where many of the Meghalayans had gathered to toast their new state. I hugged each one like a long lost friend and insisted on getting high on a Shillong favourite, Honey Bee Brandy, avoiding all the Scotches, wines and pricey liqueurs.

Once the car dipped into the lower part of town the small pretty cottages gave way to officious cantonment buildings and then to the ultimate depressants, ill kept government establishments that resembled old cardboard cartons hurriedly put together. I closed my eyes and listened to Elvis singing, 'Everybody's so lonely baby/Everybody's so lonely, they could die.'

"Robert," I said, leaning forward, putting my chin on the back of the front seat, where I should have been sitting if I wasn't so confused and so completely out of sorts.

"Yes, Kong?"

"Robert you know who killed Suresh don't you?"

The answer had no voice because it didn't need one.

23

"So, how is it going?" she asked lowering the volume of the television, her lily white breasts almost spilling out of her new nightgown.

He winced and wished he hadn't splurged on the lingerie on his last visit to New Delhi. He had to, however, because he was trying hard to impress the boutique owner, the girlfriend of a real estate don, whose voluptuousness was, to him, unparalleled. At the party, later that evening, she let him hold her close. He had spent twenty-five thousand rupees in her boutique. And why not? The deal had just been signed and his wallet felt heavy… and his heart, too, for some strange reason.

"Can't say in these matters," he replied wistfully thinking of the Delhi boobs as he started undressing. "Even if I become CM how do I solve the problem?"

"How does it matter? We'll enjoy ourselves for a few years..."

"Yeah?"

"Ok, months. And at least they'll say he was a CM once. God is great. I could never imagine this day would come. Imagine! I almost married Winston. Imagine! He is still where he was—a village school teacher."

"That's life. Winston—with a name like that—is still where he is and I—Justice—am on the verge of reaching the top... most unjustly."

"What Jus?" she asked, absorbed once again in the delights of television, the joke lost on her.

He went back to the drawing room and dialled a number. He thanked God for giving him a dim and gross woman. There was never anything to worry about.

24

THE TRAFFIC INCREASED. We slowed down. We were, by then, parallel to the Garrison Ground where we used to have our Annual Sports Day. The Civil Hospital had acquired a brighter face while the State Central Library retained its prosaic and sombre look, looking quite out of sorts opposite the elegant Church of England with its so very English face. I observed all this but in my heart my question stood waiting for Robert's answer, which did not come. Robert was like that. No one could ever shove him around. He had his own pace. Aibor was the more easy one, always relaxed and cheerful. I started missing both Aibor and Aila terribly as the car took a turn.

The Meghalaya Secretariat flashed past in pink and gray and then came Rap's Mansion and the DC's court, both bustling for different reasons. Soon Ward's Lake came into view and my eyes misted over. I gazed at the lake; a few boats lounged languidly on one side for the holiday season was over. Scattered on the slopes was, to me, an unfamiliar sight, groups of scruffy boys lazing, kind of incongruous but what the hell, it's their land and if they wish to pretty up the landscape—fine. If they don't want to do so that's also fine. What the hell?

I asked Robert to park to one side. I looked at the lake for a long, long time. There were always two or three suicides there every year, mainly lovers. That was the time when love was worth dying for. At that moment I was thinking of Kmie U Flin's love for the two boys, her 'Sures and Rabi'. I felt good just knowing that somewhere goodness still existed.

"Robert, you know who killed Suresh don't you? Who is it Robert?"

"I did … as much as you did."

"I want to meet Ravi, Robert." But even as I blurted out the words I knew my timing was wrong.

25

"RIBOK HAS CROSSED the border."

"Good."

"Badly bitten by mosquitoes, leeches he warded off with tobacco and salt, yeah, he wore long, tight socks."

"Was he alone?"

"No, Kong Jlah and her gang were there. They had gone for their maal."

"Any reaction from the Delhi woman about the arrest?"

"No, not so far."

"Good. Keep tabs anyway."

"When is she leaving?"

"She has to meet Kong Aila."

"Does she?" the question hissed through the air and hung around unanswered.

Strong sipped his beer for it was hot and humid. He was deep in thought.

Ksan slumped into a chair and lit a cigarette.

26

I KEPT STARING AT the lake, waiting for Robert to say something, knowing very well that it wasn't going to come easy. My eyes climbed up the slope to the Shillong Club established by British planters and officers in the early part of the twentieth century. It was a beautiful club with a green roof and wooden rooms. That was the club we all used to go to and dance—Aila and me and our friends—whenever the Mess didn't have a do and my family could escape the Army crowd and meet the local gentry. Often we would walk down to the lake and stroll along its moon-washed waters. Those were days when even holding hands in stolen moments was the height of delicious intimacy. The lake was dug and constructed under the supervision of a Colonel Hopkins and eventually named after the Chief Commissioner of Assam, Sir William Ward. The local people call it Nan Polok (Polok's lake) after the convict who did most of the digging. Or so I was told.

"The old club was so beautiful. Remember Robert?"

"It burnt down."

"I know but they could have replaced it with something better than this scowling monstrosity."

"There's ugliness everywhere," he said as the road curled down coquettishly to the Polo Ground and into the Golf Links.

My heart began to hammer. I was getting somewhere. Somewhere as far as Robert was concerned, somewhere also to a place, a part of the universe I loved and cherished. The eighteen hole golf course, situated at 4,750 feet above sea level was reputedly the highest in the world, a chunk of emerald spread out with pine trees all around. But when I reached there my heart sank. There was barbed wire fencing all around, houses had mushroomed all along the parallel road and people strolled around casually on the links as if it was a forgotten park.

"Robert you know who killed Suresh, don't you?"

Silence, silence and more silence.

"Don't you think you should tell the police?"

"No."

"No?"

"No."

"Why?"

"It has nothing to do with the police."

"A murder has been committed and you think it has nothing to do with the police?"

"Yes, it has nothing to do with the police, it's not a crime."

"Do you know what a crime is, Robert?"

"A forbidden act punishable by law according to the dictionary."

"So?"

"See, words and definitions in the dictionary apply to normal life. Let's say there are others who have a different dictionary."

"Oh! And in their dictionary this is not a crime huh!"

"No. Crime is not understanding another person's pain, not having the courage to accept the cause of suffering of that person's pain and not doing anything about it. That is a crime."

"And you think Suresh and co are the representatives of the criminals?"

"No, Kong, no. Didn't I say earlier that they are the punching bags?"

We were sitting on a slope in the Golf Course sharing a packed brunch of Richmond ham sandwiches. With my stomach just nicely full my heart brimmed over with confidence. I, therefore, dared to take one of Minna Jaiswal's numerous pieces of advice—take on life, face it head on and never be evasive. The more one hid the more one would be found.

"Robert, why the hell don't you all just change to a patrilineal society? Why can't...."

"WHAT? Kong, how can we? Can you, one fine day, just decide to become matrilineal? Each one of us belongs to a kur, a clan like your gotra. In one generation we cannot ..."

"Yes, sorry I understand. We cannot change all that. You can't. There is the question of who you can marry, who you cannot etc... like our gotra..."

"Kong," it was almost a whisper. "There is a war going on, a silent war."

"A disgusting war, Robert, a coward's war. Killing innocent people surreptitiously. How can you be part of it?" I was shouting.

"It's just a different kind of war, Kong. The act committed is merely a statement," he persisted, still in whispers. It was scary but I was not going to let that stop me from speaking.

"Robert, you are odious," I, too, lowered my voice to a whisper. Shouting is a sign of weakness.

"We don't expect people, all the people to understand. How can you all when our own mothers don't?"

"Huh?"

"Nobody wants to disturb the status quo, nobody wants to be flung into a state of discomfort. Comfort is happiness isn't it Kong? They would do anything for it."

"Yes, Robert, This time I cannot refute your statement. People sell themselves, their wives and their children to be comfortable. They do equate comfort with happiness. They would do anything for it. Faraway in a city in the North a beautiful aunt of mine had to sleep with a hideous

Judge. Thereafter her husband won an important land case. Everybody was comfortable.... and happy after that."

"So, Kong, like you have understood that, one day, you will understand this too, inshallah."

"What? Did I hear you say..."

"Yes, inshallah. I like this word. I learnt it from my Muslim friends. Two of them and their families have converted to Islam. Their fathers are dkhars from Bangladesh."

"Really?"

"Yes, so many others too. That is yet another story."

"Robert let us just stick to one story now. When you are ready please tell me who killed Suresh and why and also why are you protecting the killers? You will tell me won't you Robert?"

"Inshallah," and he walked towards the car and got in.

27

"Bah Jus, we've done everything now—killed, burnt, lied, cheated—what next?"

"Think boys, think, this CM has to go. Then we'll move." Jus Lamare adjusted his tie and put his hands inside the pockets of his dark gray trousers, part of his get-up for the day. The blue blazer was a Pierre Cardin, which his son-in-law, a doctor in England, had presented him for Christmas. He paced up and down the room resembling a well-preserved glamour boy rather than a high profile politician.

"Let's expose his profligacy," roared Strong, sipping his whisky.

"Yes, he has a love child from a young girl living somewhere in a village near Upper Shillong."

"So?" Jus Lamare suddenly turned, hands still in pockets, as if he was on the ramp, modelling his vanity.

"There are love children everywhere. Every Khasi child is born legitimate. Legitimacy is every child's birthright. That is the rule of our tribe since time immemorial."

"Yes, but not from a woman from the wrong clan?"

"Huh?"

"Yeah."

"She's not a Lamare."

"Yes but apparently her clan and the Lamares are forbidden to marry. She comes from a sub-clan of the Lamares. I forget the name."

"Then, that's it boys!" Jus said. Then turning to the sobbing boy he continued, "She is your cousin huh? I understand how you are feeling. But, son, once you join the Movement you have to think only for its good. That is very important. We will obviously compensate you handsomely for your sacrifice." The words fell easily like water from a tap.

Ksan went to the toilet, sat on the WC and sobbed.

28

IT FELT STRANGE and exhilarating to be soaking in the lambent light of a Shillong evening, breathing pine-scented air, thinking of the past, and coping with the present. Two different worlds, so far apart, never to meet. The past so different it seemed a separate lifetime, almost.

Then suddenly Robert spoke, "My father left Mei for a younger woman. We all felt embarrassed, abandoned and insecure. My brother started taking hash and gradually graduated to stronger stuff. I didn't mind. When he boozed it was worse, he was so aggressive. It used to frighten me. Pa died after two years, two years after he left us. He died in an accident. We were grateful. It was easier to cope."

Either Robert did not know who his real father was or he was hiding the fact from me. I didn't want to touch the subject, such an irrelevant subject.

"How did your mother cope?"

"She just carried on. Not a word of remorse or protest. She had a tea stall very close to Pine Grove School. She did good business with all the ayahs and drivers who used to come and pick up the children. Some teachers had a daily order with her for their lunch. She was so good with her tea and snacks that one of the Pine Grove parents who was establishing a Nursing Home asked her to move and manage the canteen. She did it and that gave a big boost to our finances. My brother and I assisted Mei most enthusiastically. We prospered; we bought a new fridge, a colour TV, a fancy cassette player. My mother realized one of her dreams and admitted my sister to one of the better English Medium schools in Malki. All three of us could have studied in a medium priced school but you know, we didn't think of it, our brains are so fried up, so bloody fried up."

I knew I was getting somewhere and I asked Robert to continue.

"With this newfound comfort, my brother recovered, kicked his drug habit and did his Matric privately. He's now a primary school teacher in Mawphlang. Remember Mawphlang Kong?"

"Yes, Captain Hunt's Cherry Brandy and the fascinating Sacred Groves, preserved for thousands of years to protect the environment. How could I forget?"

"Well, life went on. I used to feel pangs of jealously whenever I dropped Christine to school but I kept them to myself. I was young and as boys we didn't expect to get the best, be it education or whatever. Everyone else seemed very happy that the daughter of the house was getting the best of everything. Then one day, it was Christmas Eve and Mei was working extra hard on some special orders and my sister was in her room laughing and chatting with her friends trying on her new dresses. As I was looking at my present—a 500 rupees watch—Mei asked me to come and help her in the kitchen. Something inside me snapped. I walked into the kitchen and broke everything I could lay my hands on. Next morning Bah Aibor's parents came and took me away. They bought a taxi for me and I began to drive and earn. I liked it but, honestly, it was too much of a rough and tough job for me. My aunt, Bah Aibor's mother, realized this and before I could break more things she requested me to accompany Aibor and live with him in his new house or, rather, Kong Aila's house. She is the only daughter, so he had to move there. They are all wonderful people. They asked me to choose what kind of work I wanted to do. Well, now I manage all their affairs—the home, the vehicles, the accounting of all the various businesses, I drive. I like driving most of all. I am comfortable but it doesn't solve the problem Kong, it doesn't,"

"I am afraid I don't understand, Robert."

"There are a few intelligent, thinking guys who have started a movement to change the system to tell people here to value their sons. Nobody listens. Poor Suresh. Such a good kid."

He was quiet for a while and then he said, "Kong, we must save Ravi. It wasn't him."

29

"THE EXPOSURE WILL take a few days. Let's find all the details and do a proper job… where did he meet her, how did it happen, how old is the child. God! Imagine fathering the child of a clanswoman. What sacrilege!"

"Sub clan. That was how he goofed. Anyway, before that let us give it another shot. We cannot be silent. Nothing will be solved."

"We've already organized that."

"Great," grunted Strong and lit a cigar.

"I am glad you are in a good mood," Ksan commented.

"Aah! Of course I am. I had a great night with Allie."

"Allie who?"

"I don't know and who cares, the Boss arranged it all for me."

"We should not have chosen Bah Aibor's house…"

"The Boss wanted it. He was very sure about it. He wanted the incident to take place in a high-profile home so that the crime would get noticed. He was also very clear that he wanted it to look like a breakdown of law and order not just ethnic cleansing, that was why the robbery bit was staged…"

"Not very clever, were we, to let the other boy go?"

"Didn't want to kill two. No need. No, he won't want his whole family sent to hell would he? He won't sneak Ksan, relax, it had to be done and you know why."

"I don't know, Strong, I don't know. I can't get over the last meeting. God! That was too much, just too much."

"It had to be done… the killing had to be done. We can't have traitors. We had to show the rest that it can happen to them. We had to convey this to every one, rich and poor, big and small."

"Not the rich, certainly not the rich. How are they bothered, Strong? Their children get on anyway. Their futures are secure. Their education—the best possible—is assured and meticulously planned by their well connected parents. They are, believe me, totally unaware of the problems here. A nephew of mine studying in Hyderabad asked me, during the last bandh, what the fuss was all about. Before I could answer, a niece studying in Shimla replied, 'I swear—what's the fuss all about. Anyway, who cares?' it was as simple as that. I chanced upon them and it was an eye opener."

"Till we find an answer, let us kill some, burn some and cheat some. Oh boy! Yeah let's kill some."

"Stop it, Strong. Stop it, don't make it... worse. DON'T." But Strong wouldn't stop.

"I won't I won't. I can still recall those secret meetings at his house. So full of hope—we were demanding things for our own University. We genuinely thought it was the highway to the stars. We were as thrilled just sitting with the Boss in the drawing room, drinking good whisky, feeling sophisticated and committed. We thought the Boss was great, he was God, the Saviour who had come into our miserable rudderless lives to help us realize our dreams and lead us to a bright future. We didn't know, innocent and idealistic young idiots that we were, that he was merely recruiting us as his private army, which he could use to further his own dream and his political career. I feel strange saying all this

Ksan. I am not feeling good hearing myself speak the truth. Imagine, we actually thought the Boss was our saviour, that he was a good and selfless man. Imagine! Two decades have passed Ksan—two long decades. Twenty summers with the length of twenty long winters as Wordsworth would say. Look at our protruding bellies and thinning hair."

"Yes, yes..."

"Don't look so resigned Ksan. Looked inside your screwed up mind and your heart and your spirit. What is left of you and me? We are just pitiable insects, which he drags out when he needs to. Strike little serpents strike, strike, strike... Then when his objective is achieved he herds us back into our cells."

"Strong, this young generation... they are cleverer. Maybe they won't let him drag them around, not for too long. He will have to perform..."

"Hah! He will get his way, he always does, 'Lots of money is coming in boy! So what's the problem? Just be more generous with your time, your heart and your head' and Ksan it needs just two notes to cover the eyes. He knew, that bastard knew that and now he controls everyone in this state—ministers, bureaucrats, cops, businessmen—and us… everyone… everyone. That scum and his ilk control the destiny of our land… Oh! Ksan…"

"Strong let us do something. Let us plan something, a better strategy; let us dream a better dream, at least something truly beneficial. Let us benefit from something, somewhere. We can't let the kids be fooled like this. We have to tell… well… guide them. I feel terrible."

"What new strategy huh? Just advise them to be very sure that the Boss and the smaller bosses stick by them. Otherwise once they become ministers and have used these kids and sucked votes out of wide-eyed hapless victims like vampires, going voo voo voo in their vehicles, red lights flashing, they'll very very gently push these kids out, so gently they won't even know. Look at us, did we ever imagine in our wildest dreams that we'd forever remain like this—what would we call ourselves?—pathetic assholes too have a name you know. Say something, Ksan!"

"Ok, so we are the Boss' stooges, so what? We have not reached the top but our conscience is clear, we have not lied to anyone, we have not cheated the public. We followed orders."

"We have not cheated anyone? Our hands are soiled with the blood of innocents and you say we have not cheated and lied?"

"It's a war, Strong. In war the blood of innocents flows but we never promised them, the youth, any sort of paradise. There are no broken promises, no shattered dreams"

"God, Ksan, you really surprise me. We damn well promised by simply carrying out all these orders of the Boss who is forever giving speeches filled with promises. All clever talk to fulfil his own dreams."

"Strong, stop it, don't get carried away. Please...."

"Ksan, God! All I can see are red lights flashing voo, voo, voo, cheery waves, and friendly grins. 'We are the saviours. We will protect you all from your lands being taken, your women being raped, your spirit being crushed.' Inside, their minds are blank, their souls are jammed, they don't care a damn."

"Stop it!"

"Tell me Ksan, tell me what's the difference between the earlier rulers, the British, the Assamese... Indians and this gang? It's all the same. Can't you see they are all the same? And they are trying to say it isn't. It's all about the powerful versus the powerless."

"The dkhars, well, whatever you may say, they looked down on us."

"Ah! Don't make the mistake. The Boss and co don't look up to us either... they don't consider us equals. And when all the outsiders have fled or have been got rid of under this false pretense, when these starry-eyed kids start to wonder, when they can no longer drown their fears in whisky, drugs and sex, then whose blood will it be that will flow in the bloody rampages? Whose blood Ksan, whose blood?"

"Don't! Strong, stop it! You are talking like a madman!"

"All those dearly paid for hopes will have to be appeased. They will be like angry demons... they have to be appeased. Some one has released the virus and we have created our own Armageddon, Khasi will destroy Khasi. The process has already begun. Once an idea takes root in the mind, the process begins."

Ksan looked at his friend and he knew he had snapped. He's lost it, he thought.

The phone rang. Ksan picked it up and, for some reason, closed his eyes tightly.

"The Boss wants to meet us near the lake, first bridge. He'll be in a white Maruti van."

"Asshole."

30

As we drove in through the gate and down the slope I could see the house crouching like a huge, slumbering, dinosaur. Tall pines stood sentinel on either side and hydrangeas of mauve and pink sat eloquently on the gentle slopes. It was the season of mists and spectacular sunsets.

I saw, as the car purred down to the porch, that the gardener's cottage had its lights on.

"Robert, there's someone in the cottage. Look, lights!"

"Hmm..." he muttered casually but turned immediately to look towards the cottage.

"I am going down to see. How long can I keep pretending nothing's going on and stay out of this? "

He followed me. I could feel his sullenness with each step he took. Soon I saw Kmie U Flin, waddling out of the front door with another middle-aged woman who was neatly dressed in a gray and blue jainsem. My eyes quickly took in the gray flowers on the navy blue background and the matching blue merina topmohkhlieh covering her head, long gold earrings with blue glass drops brushed against her neck and on her feet, she wore a pair of neat black sandals with low heels. She reminded me so much of Christina, my favourite Khasi maid, and my spirits lifted a little. The third person was Titi.

The voices grew louder as they got closer. Kmie U Flin's voice was clear, upbeat and excited.

"Keep the mud from the front of the house in the small bag and the one from the back in the bigger one so that we will be able to identify. Careful, careful don't slip. Titi, are you sure you took the mud from the foot of the front steps? That's where the killers must have definitely stepped. Oh! ho! How could this happen? Poor Rabi! Poor Sures! Waw! Waw!" Kmie U Flin burst into tears.

Kmie U Flin was getting more and more hysterical. Then the other voice took over.

"Be brave, Pli. We will definitely get the killers. I have told Bah To that we would like to consult the Mussalman as well. I believe he is very powerful and also accurate in his readings. We will get to the bottom of this, don't worry."

I stepped out from behind the azaleas, out of the shadows and, light-heartedly made a face to scare them. They started laughing, Titi giggled. They seemed grateful for the small reprieve.

"Kong Raseel this is my cousin, Kong Bonili. She has come to help us solve the murder," said Titi excitedly.

"Khublei Kong Bonili, it's so kind of you to come and be with us... but, actually one is not supposed to be roaming around the scene of the crime. The police will get angry Kmie U Flin."

"We are not just roaming around Kong Raseel. We are also going to try and find out who has committed this crime." She said it all in one breath with a twinkle in her eye and somewhat uncharacteristic firmness in her tone. All that before she burst into tears again and Kong Bonili gathered her protectively in her arms.

"Now, now, stop crying, Pli. Stop it, stop. We are going to catch the killers. Bah To has never failed. Never."

"Bah To?" I was surprised. "Who is he—a private detective? If he is he should be here himself."

"Bah To is a nongpeit. He will tell us exactly what happened. He will know everything from the mud we are carrying, their towels and the hair the boys have left behind in their comb. Well, one of them has."

"You broke into the cottage?" I was horrified.

"Indeed not, but there is one... er... window they did not seal...."

I gave up as Titi burst into nervous giggles once again.

"Well, all right, how is the hair going to help Bah To?"

It soon became clear that the two women were going to seek the assistance of a nongpeit, a tantric soothsayer. He would check the mud and the hair they had brought and then with eggs, roosters and rice, unravel the mystery and then advise further.

"Please let me come with you. When are you going?" I pleaded.

I had heard of crystal gazers in London and similar soothsayers all over North India.

"We are leaving the house at 6 am come what may." Again that determined tone surfaced in the old lady's voice.

"I'll be up at five. I'll make my own tea. In fact I will make tea for everyone."

"No, no. I'll be up. I'll do that and I also need a cup of tea right now."

I was feeling rather excited walking beside the two ladies who were chattering in Khasi about esoteric remedies.

Then as we entered the kitchen and were settling down Robert staggered in. I stared at him and I could feel the blood slowly draining from my face. His eyes were blood-shot, red with anger and despair. My hand stretched out towards him. He shrank back.

"Kong Raseel, you want to go and hunt down the murderers? Don't waste time. How many will you hunt down? They are everywhere. In each of us. Once you think of something it takes life, Everything begins from thought. The very thought is the act."

31

THE GRAY WATERS of the man-made lake lay placidly under a heavy monsoon sky. The hills around gleamed with the freshness of a just-gone shower and the trees were still shaking off the drops. On one side of the iron bridge that spanned a gaping gorge a white Maruti van was parked. Very soon an old Willis jeep came bouncing down the hill road with a trailer full of loaded sacks. Freshly made brooms stuck out from all sides of the worn out trailer. Two young men, one at the wheel and one in the front seat next to him, chewed kwai purposefully but in complete silence. Only their eyes moved as they scoured the hillsides, the river beds and the scattered clumps of trees. Then the driver looked into the rearview mirror, settled it just right and as they neared the stationary Maruti, he slowed down and then stopped.

"Everything all right?" he shouted loud and clear, quite unnecessarily so.

A head stuck out.

"No, something is wrong with the car. Can you help out?"

The driver of the jeep got down and slid into the front seat of the car, next to the driver. His companion walked to the bridge and lit a cigarette, all the time scouring the countryside through small, slit eyes. The driver of the jeep then got down and opened the bonnet of the car, tinkered for a while and got into the car again. In the back seat two men in dark glasses sat, middle-aged with receding hairlines and bulbous booze-red noses, their lips crimson with pan stains and a hundred lies.

After a short while the young man slid out to the car.

"I think it should be all right now."

The whole operation took exactly fifteen minutes, as the landscape darkened further and the clouds looked ready to drop.

The man walked to his jeep. His companion joined him from the bridge.

The Maruti van sped away along the dam with a view of the lake through a lattice of leaves. It went as far as the village of Sumer. Once the road dipped into a lonely stretch the car reversed and took the road back to Shillong. The jeep was not far behind but instead of continuing straight down towards Sumer it turned left where the dam ended. The road it took had luxury farm houses dotting the landscape on one side and the freshly cut hillside on the other, gaping red like unwashed meat.

The jeep stopped a little beyond the stretch. The two young men unloaded the sacks and let them roll down the forested slopes. The sacks burst open as small stones tumbled out and disappeared into the tall grass. The two men sat quiet and still and lit a cigarette each and stared ahead at the emerald hills silhouetted against the sky, now changing colour with the falling light. A single star flickered, like a solitaire, alone, sure of its dominance.

"Ksan, the Boss conveyed two things. August 15 is approaching so we have to step up our activities. He has given half the money. He couldn't siphon too much money from the canning factory project."

"How come?"

"That nosey journalist, Irene, she brought it up in her column so the whole process has slowed down. Anyway, nothing to worry about, the funds will be pouring in. I've got a list—here it is. The name of the minister whose house will be attacked, the number of vehicles to be burnt, the localities where we create havoc. The accent is not on communalism but on the breakdown of law and order. The boss's house is also a target. He won't be there. His sentry can be dispensed with if necessary."

"Huh?"

"Obviously—it's an eyewash so that the boss will be far far from suspicion. We have to see to it—ever since Irene revealed—obliquely—the possibility of his involvement during the last carnage he has to be doubly careful...."

"I don't like this name on the list—the one whose house is...."

"Why?"

"Come on, he's a good guy. He works so hard for his constituency. He's not even that corrupt...."

"Precisely. I think the Boss detests him for all this. In fact, that's what it is. He's the one blocking the Boss' climb to the pinnacle. And of course, there's that woman Irene who makes the dumb public focus with her damned articles. Anyway, first things first..."

"Did he say anything about the... investigation... the Bihari boys."

"No. He has organized everything obviously. How could you even ask? Hah!"

"At the moment we have to focus on August 15, Independence Day. We have a major statement to make. At the meeting we have to tell the students to call for a bandh on the 14th and 15th. We have to impress upon them that the government cannot deliver and this is just the beginning. We stick to our demands. Boss will see that the CM and the cabinet do not give in. If we stretch this operation long enough, the government will fall and then Boss will have a damn good chance."

"How the hell can he influence anyone when he is in the Opposition?"

"He has his ways. Everyone has a price Ksan, grow up! Next, the dkhars are not to be attacked."

"Huh?'

"He said the headlines should shriek—'Youth fed up with government'. The rest of the work the media will do, stressing on the Reservation policy..."

"Khasi and Jaintias 60 per cent, Garos 30 per cent and others 10 per cent. Do you really think it's okay?'

They had reached the top of the ridge where they could see the town spread out beneath them, its lights glowing like a million fireflies. They sat there journeying through invisible moments in their pasts, recapturing stories.

"Strong, let's forget all that for a while. Look at that star, let's make a wish."

"All right. I wish I was back in college again sitting under those pine trees with a girl friend, singing. Humming. The pine needles are falling softly on our heads and I am dreaming of becoming a government officer like my father. Dreaming of making a life with my love, dreaming of a house with a white gate with a cat sunning itself on the front steps, contentedly licking its paws. I can almost see the roses and geraniums and orange trees, in the back garden, laden with fruit. I wish… I wish Pa had not left us. If he hadn't, my life would have been different Ksan. I wish I could raze the town to the ground and begin all over again…."

"What would your newfound world be like?"

"What would my newfound world be like? Well, let's see. Beautiful. A truly beautiful dynamic place where everyone has a job. Dynamic, developed, with its distinct identity, lots of industries, lots of productivity, green hills terraced with slopes full of crops, trees dripping fruit, rivers and streams teeming with fish, neat tin-roofed houses, complete families inside, healthy in mind and body. Mei serving us our favourite dish of rice and beef stew… I can taste it Ksan, I can taste the cabbage boiled just right and the meat. Mei just knew how to do it right… Pa would still be with us quiet as ever but out of that stillness emanated all the security that we needed. God! How could he just ditch us like that—just walk from one house to another as if he was visiting. But that's what a Khasi man is, right? A visitor in his wife's house. He gifts the woman his semen…"

"Stop it, Strong. Just keep talking positive while I roll another joint. No drinking today… go on."

"I see myself in a huge office with a circular table in front… lots of papers and pens on it, two telephones. I got the job that I deserved. I am a man of authority and position, suited and booted. I live in a home where my wife and kids respect me."

"Here's the bend Strong, pray. Come on, A Blei Trai Kynrad…"

"Ksan, don't you understand what I really want? I want my youth back. I want to live all over again."

"Pray, Strong, pray."

"For what? For the impossible?"

Then Strong sang, "Yesterday is dead and gone and tomorrow's out of sight/It's so sad to be alone/Help me make it through the night."

He sang softly, his head moving to the tune, his eyes swimming with the words.

Ksan started the jeep and moved into the enveloping darkness of the night. Strong kept singing, pleading to the wind. He thought of his little son, Badon, in his one year old grave and wished with all his heart that he was lying beside him.

32

I WOKE TO THE sound of a true monsoon morning, the music of pouring rain, the colour, the fragrances, the feel entering every nook and corner of the house. Wafting past my memory like silent ghosts was the smell of the dark, musty corridors of Loreto, our school, in the season of the rain. I could almost feel the warmth of the gray, red rimmed sweater underneath the blazer of darker gray emblazoned with the school crest Maria Regina Angelorum/Cruci Dum Spiro Fido.

As the rain continued to come down in sheets of gray and white I also remembered an unusual winter spent in the plains of Assam. December 1967 it was. I remember it had rained like this then. The Brahmaputra crossed the danger mark near a place called Dibru Darhand. We were staying in a Guest House and it become so cold that I had to resort to my school blazer. I had taken my school uniform down to take farewell photographs with my Assamese school friends.

I had never experienced rain like that and the memory stayed with me for a long, long time.

Kmie U Flin arrived with a cup of steaming hot tea. I had asked for readymade tea without the cluttered tray. She had made it perfectly, of course, just a hint of Darjeeling put in before straining for that special aroma. She was all set and ready to go, to brave the weather and meet the soothsayer who, she was quite sure, would unravel the mystery of the missing youth

"No point in delaying as this rain won't stop for many days," she predicted.

She was right and her firm decision prevailed in spite of strong protests from Robert and milder ones from Kong Bonili and a shivering Titi who was more scared than cold. Kmie U Flin stepped out into the rain, swinging her printed Made-in-China umbrella with determination.

We drove silently through the downpour. I lowered the window and the water filled my eyes, blinding me, its spray making my hair curl, its touch caressing my hand. It was as if I was in a dream. Robert was at his surliest best, his face white and still. He drove through the rain with ease, the road was as familiar to him as the weather. The car climbed up a steep slope beyond Happy Valley to stop suddenly amidst tall sal trees that grew in strange incongruity in the pine-scented forest. The rain continued to beat its musical dirge. In the depths of the forest sat a cottage of logwood, tin roofed and stone mounted. I inhaled the air through the car window, letting my hair and face get wet, dreaming of long ago, Sunday walks in Ashes Forest. By then Kong Bonili had waded bravely to the cottage with Kmie U Flin. They were going to find out when we could consult Bah To. Robert kept sitting in the car drumming his fingers on the steering wheel, humming and looking straight ahead.

I do not recollect how long it took for I suddenly heard the car door slam. Kmie U Flin was raving and ranting and Kong Bonili was consoling her. I looked at Robert. He was still looking straight ahead but his humming had stopped and he was silent and listening. Kmie U Flin was howling, the nongpeit had refused to take up the case. There were only two other clients waiting but he had refused. She was furious. We were now heading for Laban, Shillong's oldest locality, spread on the high slopes beyond the Garrison Ground.The Muslim Baba's house was just above the little market. It had green walls and a wooden green gate that seemed to have weathered many a monsoon. The Baba sat cross-legged in his prayer room, decorated with gaudy pictures of mosques. He listened attentively, nodding his head now and again understandingly. The two plastic bags with the mud, the comb and hair and two used still-damp towels recovered from the bathroom were placed by Kong Bonili in front of the Baba. He first took one towel (Suresh's I discovered later) and held it with both his hands, blew into it, muttering, and then he said, "This one is dead. He died a violent death for no fault of his." Ignoring Kmie U Flin's lachrymose response he picked Ravi's and repeated the procedure after which he said, "This one is in deep trouble. He may also die. Yes give me the mud and I will try and tell you who did it and how and why it happened."

A young boy who was obviously an assistant of the Baba brought two glasses of water. He went outside and filled the water from the garden tap. The glasses were then placed in front of the Baba who muttered a mantra and put some mud from the first plastic bag (marked 1 by Titi to indicate that it was from the front of the house) into a glass. Then everything happened all at once, the quiet chants grew louder, the water in the glass turned red and I gasped and fainted. Kong Bonili screamed 'waw' 'waw' to express shock and agony and I went numb with fear. My teeth started to chatter uncontrollably as suddenly Kmie U Flin rose up, her eyes glazed and fixed straight ahead. The baba put a knife on her head and blew on it and said "The spirit of the dead boy is inside her. He will tell you what you want to know. You can also ask him any questions you wish to ask."

I felt nauseous and my whole body felt like a block of ice. I stumbled out of the room bumping into Robert. Where had he been? Behind the door? I wouldn't know. I rushed to the car and leaned hard against it. Through half closed eyes I saw Robert rushing inside the hut. I opened the car door and collapsed on the front seat.

As always, so typical of Shillong weather, the rain suddenly let up and bright sunshine streamed through from a sky now turning deep blue and white. For a second, the world became beautiful again, a familiar world where murder occurred, for most people, only in Agatha Christie novels. I revelled in it for a while, how long I don't know, and somehow managed to divert my mind completely from the bizarre situation. The car doors suddenly slammed shut. Robert slid into the driving seat. I looked back and found Kmie U Flin was fast asleep. Next to her Kong Bonili had her eyes tightly shut. She was wide awake though. I could make that out. Something was terribly wrong. Weighed down by secrets known and unknown I started to cry.

33

INSIDE THE TALL white house with windows like hollow eyes, that rose above a cluster of hill cottages red roofed and innocent, the two men had just surfaced after a late night. Their eyes were puffy but they were alert and full of thoughts.

"Now let me get this straight Ksan, the nongpeit cooperated with us but after that they went—where?"

"To some damn Mussalman in Laban and—God—I can't begin to tell you what happened there, well according to our reliable source …"

"For God's sake just tell me…."

"The Mussalman called the spirit of Suresh Rai and it apparently told him everything …'

"No!"

"Yes, Strong, yes. Do these things really happen?"

"Well obviously they do. That's not the issue at the moment. Who was there, who heard him is what is important."

"Robert..."

"I know, I know. What about the old lady?"

"She was the medium so she wouldn't know."

"What!"

"The medium never remembers! The friend or cousin... Kong Bonilie who lives in Laitumkhrah... she heard everything but who'll believe her?"

"The point is even if the cops hear what she tells them, they will pick up the leads, they are perfect leads. Where exactly does Bonili stay? Find that out and also if there's a loyalist doctor in that vicinity—fast!"

34

During the silent drive back home from the nongpeit and the Muslim baba I reeled under the most excruciating pangs of guilt. How could I have fled during the most crucial moment at the Baba's? Why the hell had I gone if I was going to do such a cowardly and stupid thing? How could I, when I was perhaps the first and only witness to the crime? How could I when I'd already let Suresh and Ravi and Aibor and Aila down by not coming clean with the cops? How could I? How could I? But, you know, in life there comes a point when you can keep questioning yourself but there are really no answers.

Once at home, Kong Bonili and Robert took Kmie U Flin to her room. I staggered into mine and passed out. I woke up to a still house with just the tip-tip of a light drizzle. It was gray everywhere and I was famished. I went to the kitchen and made myself a huge brunch. Fried eggs sunny side up and sausages, roast chicken and mashed potato from the fridge and some bread rolls and a Cherrapunji banana, 'kait jaji', incomparable in their aroma and taste. I laid everything out on the circular dining table, the teak shining brownish black. The rose petals fallen from the vase gazed at me and I stared back at them as I ate. I felt strangely soothed, mesmerized by their fragility and stillness, like autumn leaves carpeting the earth. I never ever allow the gardener to sweep away the leaves in my little Delhi back lawn, my private haven. The meal went down my gullet and settled comfortably inside my grateful stomach. I felt better.

I was sipping a hot cup of coffee when Robert poked his head in through an open window.

"Oh! Kong, I am so glad you are eating something. I don't think Kmie U Flin can make any lunch. I can get some Chinese food or jadoh from the takeaway."

"No thanks. I've just wolfed down a good brunch. I would now like to go out for a drive."

"In this drizzle?"

"Yes."

He gave a huge smile. The brightest, happiest ever, If I'd know what lay ahead I'd have captured it on camera to illustrate the irony and travesty of life.

"By the way Kong, Bah Aibor and Kong Aila are arriving the day after tomorrow."

"That's wonderful!"

I changed my clothes; slipping out of my kaftan into a long skirt and polo neck and gathered my hair into a ponytail. Robert had brought the car out while I went to Kmie U Flin's room. Kong Bonili was sitting beside her slumbering friend and Titi was pressing her feet. I smiled at them and left.

"Robert, I want to go to the District Jail."

Silence.

"Robert, I want to go is the District Jail to see Ravi."

"Kong, why don't you wait till Kong Aila arrives? We'll have to get permission."

"I already have permission."

Of course I didn't but I just wanted to take a chance and I wasn't going to spoil it by telling Robert the truth.

The jailer wasn't a Khasi, I could make that out. He was busy having an animated conversation on the phone and quite obviously very happy. He saw me and seemed pleased at my appearance and cupping the mouthpiece asked me what I wanted. I said a little prayer and told him. He hollered for an assistant I filled up a tattered register and before I knew it I was through.

The long, black, dark corridor of the jail seemed like an endless tunnel leading straight to hell. I felt as if I was walking though the insides of a serpent. I felt, quite simply, cold and terrible but I knew I could not back out. I had to make the trip.

The cell was dimly lit with an ancient cot on one side and the walls had blankness and despair inscribed everywhere. Ravi was hunched on the cot, smoking an unfiltered cigarette.

"Ravi..."

My voice sounded strange but steady and friendly. I felt as if I knew this person well, having seen him in that one instance on that misty evening filled with horror.

"Ravi..."

Still no response.

"Ravi, I know you didn't kill Suresh." I spoke in Hindi.

The boy looked up. His eyes were filled with shock and fear. His mouth fell open, I felt faint. This was not the face I had seen. This was not Ravi.

"Why? Why? Who are you! You are not Ravi."

I got no answer as his lips pursed tightly with a kind of ominous finality that made me shiver. I felt like an intruder in a world where scores had been settled, all payments made. I walked out. The jailor was still on the phone, laughing raucously.

The rain started again and increased steadily. Soon it was coming down in torrents. The newspapers reported it as "the highest rainfall in 30 years, probably caused by the depression in the Bay of Bengal".

35

"THE WOMAN WENT to the jail."

"I know"

"She knows…"

"The Boss is deciding what to do next."

"Yeah. Good. When do we get a chance to think, as in think, anyway?"

"Thank God! The rain has let up a little. Be careful, Strong, don't slip. You've had a lot or what?"

There were not many strollers along the narrow path that rimmed the gorge just above the roaring waterfall. It was a working day and a misty morning, the ground slushy with leeches lurking in the tall grass. Inside the cave, naturally gated with two huge rocks and giant ferns, twenty or more men sat in council. Strong and Ksan entered amidst muffled greetings Khublei, Khublei, Hi, Hello, nods, hands limply raised or just silent acknowledgements.

An hour later they emerged in twos and threes with ten or fifteen minute gaps in between and scampered up the hillside confidently. Most of them knew the terrain well. For some it was a childhood haunt where they had picnicked and hunted birds with catapults. Those who were not so confident of these wooded heights were cheerfully guided by fourteen-year-old Niro. He'd grown up in these slopes and still picked mushrooms and gathered wild herbs for his mother's kitchen. Just out of habit because, unlike earlier times, now there was always meat and fish, vegetables and even fruit, all neatly stored in a brand new fridge. Niro was after all a working man, a respected member of his family and the Organization. His work was to spy, tell lies and spread rumours for the benefit of the Boss. So what, his parents thought, at least someone in the family was working and earning well. Besides isn't the Organization working for the benefit of the people?

Like the last time Niro was told to stroll casually, kite in hand and trick the police who were looking for a suspected militant.

He had overdone the details but the police were unsuspecting of the fourteen-year-old with a yellow kite in his hand and a curly mop of hair atop a smiling face. As the jeep sidled up into the lane that led to the green-roofed cottage someone threw a bomb. There was a loud, earsplitting explosion but the road still remained empty. No crowds came rushing out. The cops, caught in a situation they did not anticipate, left the scene their mission incomplete. The militant was never caught.

Soon after, Niro's parents become the proud owners of a sofa set, two beds (real wooden beds with springy Dunlop mattresses) and also a colour television. Life became almost strange, unbelievable to young Niro as he sat late into the nights transporting himself to different worlds just with the press of a button. His mother invested in lengths of flowery curtains that billowed in cream, deep pink and mint green in the mountain breeze. She had, thankfully, progressed from grim resignation to hopeful cheer after the arrival of the TV and even doubled up with laughter now and again. She started to hug and kiss Niro's younger siblings, filling their ears with unfamiliar murmurs.

Niro's father, who had been jobless for months, had, prior to this, started drinking to drown his sorrows. He had dreamt and prayed and hoped for the job in the soon-to-be constructed canning factory in the suburbs of the town. The plan was suddenly shelved however, the funds ran out they said. Same old story. It seemed Niro's father, like everyone else, knew the money must have gone towards realizing the desires and dreams of those who were privileged enough to be able to make their dreams a reality. Brand new cars, trips to exotic places with the entire family, servants in tow, gifts for the wife and children and mistresses—that was where the money always flowed anyway, diverted like irrigation water.

Niro's father, Curtis, walked out of his dream job to his mother's house. On the way he picked up his friend, Rodrik, who had suggested a plan, an encouraging alternative. Besides Rodrik was confident, articulate, a graduate, he would be able to put things across better than Niro's father. So his mother was told that a small provision store on the main road not far from his house was what they had planned to set up. He wanted a loan. His mother said she did not have so much ready cash to which Niro's father suggested that she could dispose off some of the land at the foot of the garden. He would buy it from her. He had brought with him his wife's jewellery—everything she had—as security.

His mother's impassive face suddenly twisted into a grimace. Niro's father put his hands together, fingers entwined on his slightly parted knees and let his mind go blank. Rodrick looked out of the window. Niro's grandmother popped some tobacco into her mouth and said, "I don't know what you mean? What land? You have no share in this land. What has happened to this world, sons coming to their mothers demanding money? Can this ever happen in a respectable Khasi home? What is happening? Curtis, you ask your wife to ask her family. She has only one sister. Yes, I know she married you against her family's wishes but what can I do? It was your choice. What will your sisters say? And please, son, don't trouble your father. He is not well and, anyway, this is not his property, as you know."

Niro's father's heart sank and his hands felt clammy and cold. Rodrik and he finished their tea in silence and walked out onto a nothing pavement in a nothing world. They drank themselves into oblivion in a seedy bar and, even today do not remember how they reached home.

Then, one day, Niro told them, hesitantly, that he had a job. The news was as hesitantly conveyed to Niro's mother who simply smiled and asked no questions. Niro suddenly looked grown up and developed a certain importance.

He thanked God many times and, filled with deep gratitude, actually attended church for three consecutive Sundays as did his parents.

Niro had spent the entire week all over town, in his usual haunts, telling people about the robbery and murder in Bah Aibor's house. He stuck to the orders embellishing the stories just enough to make the conversation interesting.

36

"THERE ARE TWO days left for the bandh and we're a week away from August 15th..."

"What is the slogan supposed to be?"

"You were dozing, I saw you."

"I watched a movie till 3 am. Frankly, I heard nothing."

"Ok ok. There's no slogan. They agreed on the Boss' strategy. Of course they think it's my strategy. They don't even know it is a strategy. They think it's the ten commandments straight from heaven. Same old thing... it's the reservation, inner line permit... all that he told me at the meeting at the lake. Then of course, the stress has to be on breaking away from Indian colonialism!"

"Usual Delhi bashing."

"Yeah and why not? Got reports that in the Independence Day Speech which the Prime Minister has prepared or rather which had been prepared for him there is no mention of the North East, so it's a good opportunity to come down hard."

"What? Not even Nagaland and Manipur?'

"No."

"No police bashing again, I hope. How long can we use them too as punching bags? When are we going to come out clean, Strong? We are cowards. We Khasis are cowards."

"NO, Ksan NO. And stop chattering. Stop going off track. We are coming out clean and we will go through with it, execute it meticulously… ."

"What are you talking about? Go through with what?"

"You are the limit! I don't want to spell it out. It's too dangerous. Walls too have ears you know…."

"But you have to tell me…."

"Ok let's go out, let's go for a walk to the edge of the gorge. Let the wind carry the words away."

Behind the green hills in the distance the sun was sinking into a sea of silver flecked clouds. A Shillong sunset after a heavy shower was a treat for the mind and heart. Silhouetted against it stood Strong and Ksan, almost as if they were part of the scenery.

"Strong, stop stop. We are now attacking our own blood! What are you SAYING?"

"It's a war man. All's fair in love and war. Say it once Ksan, say it once to the wind. Once it is said half the deed is done, come on."

"No, no I can't. I simply cannot sink to such a level."

"Oh yeah? It isn't as if we have never killed. By the way the old lady's cousin, Kong Bonili died of a heart attack early this morning."

"Huh?"

"She had some tea after dinner with some visitors from the locality. After that she went to sleep."

"Strong..."

"Yes?"

"We are SICK."

37

THE PHONE RANG just when I'd finished dinner. Good dinner, smoked pork cooked with onions, garlic, tomatoes and bamboo shoot and mashed potatoes sprinkled with jamyrdoh and served with red hill rice.

"Kong, thank you. This meal is out of this world," I told Aila's cousin, who had come to help with the cooking.

"Tomorrow I'll cook fish for you, elisa in mustard oil, steamed with onion, nei lieh and green chillies and pepper. It is a Bengali dish but I believe you like it very much," she answered cheerfully.

I knew they were all trying their best to keep me happy and obviously Kmie U Flin had managed to give instructions in spite of her trauma.

The phone rang. I raced for it thinking it was Aila. It wasn't.

"May I speak to Raseel Singh?

"Speaking."

It was one of Aibor's friends, a minister, Princeton Lyngwa. He said he had just come to know about my visit and he was sorry about all the trouble and the inconvenience caused by the robbery. He would like to invite me to his residence for dinner the following day. It was his wife's birthday but no presents please! Transport would be arranged.

"Anything else I can do for you, Raseel?"

"Well, yes, Bah, I went to the District Jail yesterday to visit Ravi, the suspect. I am quite sure that the young man incarcerated is not Ravi."

"Pardon? I don't quite get you."

I knew that that was not true but he was buying time for the right response. So I repeated what I had said anyway out of deference for his position and out of anxiety for my own.

"Really? This is certainly very serious. I'll look into it. I'll ring up the SP at once. Anything else? You are really quite an amazing girl."

"I don't think it's a simple case of robbery at all. In fact I am quite sure of that too."

"Raseel I am a friend of Aibor's and you are his guest. You've come for a holiday. Do you want to get involved in this mess? You don't have to feel guilty. I'll sort it out."

I kept silent. I was shocked.

"I can understand how you feel. We'll talk about it tomorrow. In the meantime I'll contact the SP straightaway."

I told Kmie U Flin about the invitation. It brought her out of her shock and grief over Kong Bonili's sudden demise. Her swollen red eyes lit up a little at the thought of my being invited by the minister. I hugged her tight. I didn't know what else to do. I had been doing that all day ever since I got the news about Kong Bonili's sudden demise. I was somewhat thankful for the natural death. Her hearing everything the 'spirit' had to say had endangered her and I was scared and miserable.

"Kong, you must wear a dress, a long dress. You will look beautiful, your hair you leave open but pin it back like Sonia Gandhi."

"Good lord! A long dress...."

"Yes. All right not so long, a mini."

"Eeks! What? I thought you said long."

"She means midi, Kong."

It was Robert.

Robert had just entered the room. Kmie U Flin looked down at her toes shyly. I hugged her again. In that one instance I felt the burden of her sadness. Great sadness of things past and things to come

"Ok a midi."

"Yes, good, Kong… a dress."

"Accha, I get you. Desi saris and salwars are not approved here. Aila had told me but I forgot. But I'm going to a private party, an exclusive gathering."

"Kong, Meisan is right. They are everywhere and watching: please wear something safe—tribal or western—best."

"I know very little about dressing. I noticed Kong Aila and I asked one day…I told her that if she wore a Punjabi dress she would look like Juhi Chawla…yes, she would."

"We are all Indians but the rest of India knows nothing about us, they call us Assamese."

"Robert, the North Indians call everyone from the South, Madrasis and when you go south, the South Indians call everyone from the North, Punjabis."

"Where does Kanodia come from Kong Raseel?"

"Kanodia is a Marwari. He comes from Rajasthan in north west India."

Kanodia owned the huge provision store from where the household procured their monthly requirements. He, like the rest of his community, owned all the large shops in Shillong along with the Sindhis, although the Sindhis concentrated on ready-made garments. Their shops stood out because of their excellent window dressing. In 1863 the British shifted their headquarters from Cherrapunjee to Shillong because of the excessive rainfall. In 1864, Police Bazaar was founded with the setting up of a departmental store, Ghulam Haider and sons. A hundred years later when I was a young schoolgirl it housed Modern Book Depot. My parents and I frequented Abdul Gaffoor and Sons, which was set up in 1872 when Shillong become the capital of Assam. I used to love going there—I loved the different soaps and their aromas, the powders, stationery, toys, handkerchiefs, biscuits, toffees, an endless array of goodies—everything except booze and cigarettes. Below Abdul Gaffoor was

Jamatullah and his tailoring shops. My first grown up no-frills dress was beautifully stitched by him. After that, they say, came the big Marwari traders and merchants, the Singhanias, the Goenkas. Some of their children were in school with us. The Marwaris were closely followed by the Bengalis who set up bookstalls and photograph studios like the Ghosal Brothers. In 1905 when Nawab Bahadur Kasimuddin started the first taxi service between Shillong and Gauhati (now Guwahati) motor workshops sprang up. Khan Motors was walking distance from our beautiful bungalow in the nearby cantonment area so we patronized the workshop quite frequently. After that we'd take the longish walk to Morello's and have a cup of tea with slices of sponge cake and the most delicious chicken sandwiches.

Kmie U Flin and Robert listened to my recounting of this history, enraptured; most locals didn't know all this but I did because I guess I loved reading and travelling and Shillong. By then I had decided what to wear. A calf length skirt, slim fit top with long sleeves, my natural coloured pashmina and cherry coloured Lotus Bawa shoes. How Delhi-girl I felt but for once it didn't feel too bad.

The phone rang. It was Aila !

"Ras, Ras how are you? We heard about the ghastly incident."

"Where are you, you crazy girl?"

"We're in Cal. From China we went all over that's why we missed the messages. No, no one messaged the details they thought it would be too much. We have just heard the news. Aibor and I felt so terrible."

"Don't worry, Aila. I've been through enough to be prepared for this. Just tell me—when are you arriving? I'm longing to see you."

"Ras, day after—positively. Aibor has some important work in Cal but he has talked to everyone concerned ...and my brothers are there to handle it. I have to be here, you know the usual boring entertainment one has to go through. Life for us business types is never easy. I am longing is get back Ras and give you a proper holiday."

"I'm rather enjoying my improper one!"

"Oh! Ras you are so full of beans. How's Kmie U Flin? She adored those boys. Oh God! That reminds me. I must get the proper prayers and rituals done in that cottage to cleanse it of the 'tyrut'."

"The what?"

"Tyrut... it's a kind of curse resulting from any violent death. It attacks generation after generation unless it is cleansed. We are Christians but we also get it done. Ras, you are so strong. I'd have run off the day after that ghastly...."

"I can't Aila, I'm too deeply involved.'

"Involved?"

"Yes, I... well, I sort of saw almost the whole crime. The boy they've locked up is not your garden help, Ravi. Aila, there is some terrible mistake somewhere. There is something very very wrong. I saw the murderers, Aila. I can even identify one... Aila?'

There was no response to my sudden outpouring. There was a silence so fierce, it gored my heart.

"Aila?'

"Yes, Ras." A whisper.

"I am sorry."

"Ras, please keep away till we come. I am really sorry."

"Aila, don't be sorry you crazy girl. You had warned me that things here are bad... just finish your work then come ok? Bye."

"Bye, Ras, listen, think about it. If you want to leave right away you can come to Cal we can meet here....'

"No, Aila let's meet here as planned."

"OK, then bye, let me know if...."

"Ok, ok, Aila. Bye."

I watched television for awhile then tried to read, making the sofa, covered in English upholstery, my bed. I don't know when I fell asleep with *The Idea of India* resting precariously on my chest.

I was shaken out of my slumber by the sound of shattering glass in my room, which was next door. As I entered it the night wind rushed in through the broken windowpanes tearing angrily at the mosquito net around my bed that had been lowered for the night. I switched on the light. On the bedside rug lay a huge stone. It had obviously failed in its mission.

I switched off the lights and went back to the drawing room. I gulped a Valium with a glass of water and fell into a deep sleep, wrapped up in a huge Naga shawl. Before I did, however, I recorded a small detail that snuggled into my mind throughout my conversation with Aila: someone was listening on the extension.

38

I FIRMLY TOLD THE entire staff, the following morning that, in spite, of the previous night's incident we were not going to do a thing until Aila and Aibor returned. Then I drove out and spent the whole morning and afternoon in the beauty parlour in Laitumkhrah. The owner of the upmarket salon treated me to chicken patties and espresso coffee from the new bakery in town and supplied me with Davidoff cigarettes from her Christian Dior bag. I returned from a most satisfying session and sank into a much-needed siesta. By seven I had showered and felt on top of the world. Kmie U Flin brought me a concoction of brandy, hot water, honey and lemon to protect me against the chills that always set in when one bathed in the evening in the hills.

I had moved up to the first floor, to a room with a different view—no orchard, no gardener's cottage but a quiet benign slope landscaped Japanese style. At the bottom was a circular pond necklaced with irises of purple and moonlight white.

I dressed with care and totally in keeping with the advice of the wise old one of the house. The SP looked appreciatively as he took my statement about the broken window in my room. I was startled by his presence in the hall as I sailed down. I glared at Robert for going against my orders but he had his duties and I understood. It was obvious, after the inspection of the grounds outside, that the intruder could not have traversed miles for he was barefoot. He must have known where to aim. It was the window closest to my bed. The SP posted two guards for my benefit and left.

I took a deep breath and tried to forget about all that.

On the way to Princeton Lyngwa's house I passed the erstwhile Polo Grounds, now a huge stadium for soccer and hockey. An eyesore if one compared it to what it had once been, a beautifully kept patch of emerald green turf for the races, encircled by wooden stiles. Races outlived Polo, the game that originated in neighbouring Manipur. During my girlhood days I used to love coming to the races because my mother would be at her sunniest best, laughing and betting with her Khasi friends. My father did not know of this delicious, surreptitious indulgence of hers. As the car dipped and then climbed up to the Minister's house I could almost hear that tinkling laughter of hers and my eyes smarted. I was grateful that the dark August night wrapped me in its cover. The darkness completely blanketed the Umkhrah stream, now no longer a sparkling hill stream full of cheer but a sluggish sewage choked with the city's filth. Does anyone even consider Nature's feelings when they indulge in such callousness? Don't they know that the wrath of Nature surpasses all great emotions? I mourned for so many things lost forever.

The enormous wooden bungalow nestled amidst a brotherhood of tall pines. The red pine verandah shone like only a Khasi floor can shine and the aroma of recent polish wafted to the car as we drove into the porch. In true Delhi style, I began to arrange my thoughts and feelings, juggled up appropriate but not bright conversation and fixed my face to a near perfect expression of delight and joie de vivre. Deep inside, of course, my heart churned with inexplicable emotions. I told Robert to go home and relax. I decided to take up the Minister's offer and get dropped home. I wanted to be as free and as far away as possible from last week's events.

As soon as the car came to a stop a tall and striking young man walked up to welcome me. I couldn't help noticing the well cut suit and inhaling the expensive cologne he wore as his handsome face split into a grin.

"Good Evening Ma'am."

"Khublei."

"Oh yes, khublei, khublei."

Khublei, kyrkhu u Blei, meant God bless you. It is the traditional form of greeting when Khasis meet each other and also while parting. It also means thank you. It was the first Khasi word we learnt when we reached Shillong. We learnt it from our first maid, Rimon.

The tall and slim young man introduced himself as the Minister's eldest son. He smiled a great deal and I could not help noticing his even teeth and healthy pink lips. His hair shone like copper. It was obvious that some time, somewhere along the line an Englishman had stormed into the family genes. Great looks, great education—Pune, New Delhi, east coast USA where he was graduating in economics the following year. One sister was doing Hotel Management in Sydney and another studying in an exclusive boarding school in Mussoorie.

We stepped into the lawn where people sat in circles around elegant tables covered in white tablecloths. Napkins, crockery, flowers, tables, chairs were all whistle clean white. Some guests stood around the bar, chatting, drink in hand. From the group the Minister walked up to me followed by his arrestingly beautiful wife, a shorter version of Catherine Zeta-Jones. He was not too bad either with his antiquated charm, which went exceedingly well with his pipe and Louis Armstrong voice. Everything seemed perfect but I was, somehow, not feeling right.

"So many guests," I heard myself say, my voice faltering. I had a feeling of unwanted inadequacy.

"Yes," the Minister's wife responded fingering her off-white pearls that matched her 'dhara', "that's Bah Ibanmanik. He is one of our ministers, also a chieftain, a syiem."

In the Khasi hills there are big states 'himas' and smaller ones 'elakas'. A hima is ruled by the syiem who is elected from the royal clan by the myntris, the ministers, who are representatives of the important clans of the 'hima'. To this day all these rulers have special administrative and judicial powers. The British did not conquer the Khasi Hills but signed treaties with the syiems.

"Come Raseel, let's go and meet him."

The waiter came by with a tray of drinks. I picked up a gin and tonic and gulped it. The minister's sister-in-law, Joyce, walked up to me and put her hand around my waist like an old friend.

"Let's not rush to meet Iban as if we are fans," she laughed. "He is damn handsome but will he hand us some?"

I doubled up with laughter at this small joke, so grateful for the respite.

Ibanmanik Sing definitely had his fans. Medium height and athletic, his bespectacled handsome face sported a moustache and an attractive mien of great confidence.

"He's a Minister, look at his strut. He walked so regally earlier but now he struts."

"Joyce, I believe the youth here, the young men especially are very dissatisfied with the system. Sad isn't it and what...."

"Yes, there's lot of trouble but what's so sad? These boys are just causing all this mayhem for lack of better things to do."

"I don't think so. I don't think so at all. The young men and women involved couldn't be enjoying it at all."

"Oh yes, they are and why not? Monsters! They are having a whale of a time, easy money, drugs or drinks-induced happiness, plenty of sex, no real responsibilities. Anyway, my husband and I are Khasis but we live faraway from this hellhole in Cal. We come twice a year to see everyone and see to our properties, we enjoy ourselves and zip off...."

I was stunned. I popped a chicken wanton into my mouth from a passing tray.

"We used to get better wantons. But now the Chinese have all left." Joyce licked her finger delicately as her diamonds glittered unabashedly.

"Why have they left?"

I wasn't really interested but I just wanted to say something as my eyes ran all over the place. I didn't know why I was feeling so uneasy.

"Victims of extortion.... that's why. For the Cause hah! Delinquents! Thank God, my kids are in Pune in decent schools, in decent company."

"Because they can afford it, Joyce. Those so-called delinquents can't."

It was just then that there was a loud commotion and two gunshots rang through the air. In a turbulence of flapping wings some resting birds rose above the trees and fled. Joyce caught my hand and started praying. Scores of policemen appeared from nowhere and converged at the gate. Two of them were obviously hurt and being led away.

It couldn't have taken long because the taste of the wanton still lingered in my mouth. The minister's son came striding towards me and holding me by the shoulders said quietly,

"Come, don't worry. It was an intruder. Yes, a Khasi. Must have been drunk but one can't take a risk."

He led me to a room where a friend's son was playing Beethoven, as if nothing had happened. A waiter brought a tray of drinks. I grabbed another gin and tonic and took huge gulps.

39

IT WAS NOON by the time I woke up and Aila was home. My spirits soared as I tumbled out of bed and quickly got ready. She looked wonderful after her holiday, Star cruising from Hongkong to Zhanjiang and then unto Halong Bay. She said, in Haikou, capital of China's Hainan Island, the 'Hawaii of the Orient', she made a wonderful discovery: that she was not as in love with her husband as she thought. A few months before the cruise she got wind of her husband's infidelity and called me up—she wept copiously and blamed it on her barrenness. In the same breath she cited umpteen examples of men who had a football team at home but yet who strayed. I sold Star Cruises to her and advised her to go find herself.

"I am all right, Ras," she said, without my asking.

Then she stretched her lithe body languidly as her Tods slipped off her small, perfect feet.

"Aila you are looking absolutely wonderful. I am so happy."

Aila's feet now rested on the mula, the ubiquitous cane stool, as her eyes roamed all over her weedy, monsoon garden, sprayed with colour by a rebellious gulmohur and a quiet jacaranda. Aila was exceptionally attractive and different. She, the daughter of an English tea planter's son and a highborn Khasi lady, had inherited her father's auburn hair and green eyes. She never ever let things get her down for long. She was good at Sports and Dramatics and also won all elocution and debate trophies. Those were the halcyon days when there was no unwritten blanket rule that all the children should shine in academics or else. If you did—wonderful—if you did not the teacher tried to find something else special within the child. Aila in spite of her continual fifty percents was a star and being of mixed blood and Catholic also helped tremendously in a convent. She knew it and had a ball throughout without ever being brash; that inimitable grace she inherited from Aunty Rosamon.

"Ras, now you tell me what happened. Or should we wait for Aibor? He rushed off straight for his office. Just grabbed some fruit and his sweater and off he went. He looked so tired.... Yeah, there's so much violence here, Ras.

If you go to a public place you can feel it in the air. A cousin of mine—you know her Adriana—she and her entire family have moved out of their ancestral home in Mawkhar."

"That beautiful home? What happened?"

"Well, one night they heard some commotion outside in the street so they switched off the lights and peeped—the usual procedure here. There was a group of boys around a dkhar boy who had fallen and they were stoning him. Blood was spurting from him but they wouldn't stop. She called the cops but it was too late. They came only to collect a mass of flesh—someone's child, brother, husband, friend, Ras. I feel so ashamed. They said they kept hearing that awful sound pchaak pchaak of some one being stoned and blood spurting out, for months on end. Can you imagine? Oh! Ras things here are bad, so bad. You can't imagine Ras…I am so ashamed of my community."

"I can Aila, I can but we'll wait for Aibor then I'll tell you. I can't do it twice."

"Oh!" She chirped and her forehead smoothened.

I knew she wasn't keen to know so I let it go. We lapsed into silence staring at the sky and beyond. Yet I was scared. Even when my parents were murdered and I returned home to a strange flat filled with incense and relatives I did not feel this cold, clammy terror. Maybe because I arrived three days later and my uncles did not wait for me to be part of the last rites because of the heat. I cried for many weeks any time, any place and shivered with the thought of the double murder but I did not feel like I felt now. Maybe because then I knew who the criminal was and who the victims were. This time I didn't.

40

"THE STONE DID not scare the Delhi woman."

"I know."

"Kong Aila and Bah have returned."

"I know. I wonder what the Boss will do next. The CM has resigned so he gets full marks there but I believe Aibor didn't get the contract to build the Amusement Park. Aibor, I believe is wild. He is fuming"

"What a scum, the Boss is.... How could he do this? Why didn't he see that Aibor gets the contract? He's been making full use of him. Even staging this whole crime in Bah's house. God!..."

"The Marwari gave thirty-forty crores or something like that."

"I heard Aibor has threatened to spill the beans."

"NO! That's so bloody dangerous... for Aibor. God!"

"I know. Shit! I'm not feeling good, Ksan."

"Nor am I."

41

LUNCH WAS SERVED in the verandah on a three tiered rosewood trolley. I tossed and turned quite a few ideas in my mind before I settled on a topic. I wanted all the questions answered, all my doubts cleared, somehow. I'd begin gently I thought, at the beginning.

"Aila your paternal grandpa fought for a separate hill state didn't he?'

"Oh yes, He didn't stand for elections and all that but he was very much a stalwart in the movement. I'll never forget the chant 'We want hill state, no hill state no rest.' We got this separate state in my last year of school—a year and as half after you left. You know it was quite traumatic for me frankly because my parents stopped me from going over to Shikha Mukherjee's. Yes, yes imagine! Just because she was a Bengali—I remember that last Durga Puja I watched the festival in her house sitting in my attic and crying. For years

I was part of it all, even Mei and Pa used to go over for the feast. Part of me was severed just like that. The Mukherjees sold the house and left and Shikha eventually finished her school from Darjeeling. She couldn't bear Cal, having grown up in the hills all her life. Some rich people from Jaintia Hills have bought the house now. It looks different, brightly painted and filled, literally flooded, with potted plants. The smells and the sounds are different. We still share the same hedge. I miss my old life, my old friends, Ras. Remember Hillaire Belloc?"

And we recited together in the now lambent light... From quiet homes/and first beginnings/Out to the undiscovered ends/there's nothing worth/the wear of winning/but laughter and/the love of friends.

It was then that we saw a fleet of cars coming down the driveway. Slowly, very slowly, they purred to a stop for what seemed like eternity, while Aila and I froze and wondered what this was all about. Nobody stepped out of the cars. Two white Marutis, Aibor's Mercedes, a Zen and a Willis jeep stopped in a straight line on the slope, still, very still. Then, first two women stepped out. I recognized one as Aila's mother's sister, Aunty Irene, Aila's father emerged next and walked down with his wife, her face so pale, geisha white. They stared at us and we stared back then suddenly Aila screamed, a scream I'll never forget, and flew into her aunt's arms. She knew, even before they told her, that she had lost the one person who she tried so hard to stop loving but failed.

Aibor was dead. He was waylaid and shot three times in the head while returning home from his office. Strangely the incident took place in such a beautiful spot, the lovely, winding road that climbs up from Polo Ground to the pine scented colony on top—the road that was the longest way home. Maybe Aibor wanted to use a different route that fateful day but why, we didn't know. They shot Robert too. Robert was also dead. Simultaneously 'Ravi Rai' conveniently managed to get hold of some poison and was found dead in his miserable cell. Suresh's body was never found.

The sudden unexpected turn of events, the enormity of the tragedy completely shattered me. I knew for certain that this time I would not be able to cope.

That night I rang up Renu Masi and Vinny. The following day Vinny and her fiance Vijay arrived. They stayed for the three days' mourning period. They did all they could to help Aila get over the loss of a husband and me for the loss of a world I had clung to for so long and, now, no longer knew.

They knew it was a world I needed to return to again and again to maintain my sanity. They knew the loss was as great as Aila's.

Aibor was dead. I couldn't even say 'hello' after so many years of not seeing him. From the airport he'd just come, picked up his sweater and gone straight to 'work'. Aila came home to be with me, to participate in what now seemed a perfect epilogue, her eyes filled with the secret knowledge that she could not share. I had noticed that and felt strange and sad for it was so unlike Aila. The falseness had hung on her like an ill-fitting gown. I watched her from a distance amidst flowers and condolences, breaking down now and then filling the house with cries of despair, which broke my heart again and again.

Aunty Irene, Uncle Don, her husband and almost a dozen relatives had moved in for the mourning period. Aibor's body lay in a tent outside while the locality boys and male relatives kept vigil all night. Since he died an unnatural death his body was not brought inside the house. I didn't even see Robert for he was taken straight to his mother's place. I don't want to write about the deaths. I had said good-bye the night before, to everyone, in my mind. To Robert too, I said good-bye the night before. I wrote down Hillarie

Belloc's poem and put the paper on Aibor's cold chest and sent one to Robert too through a relative.... From quiet homes/and first beginnings/out to the undiscovered ends/there's nothing worth/the wear of winning/but laughter and/the love of friends.... I loved them both in different ways for, like me they were people in pain, pain that would now continue for many more lifetimes. And they were both my childhood friends and, to me, wonderful men caught in circumstances beyond their control, as they played out their own karmic games. Maybe they were wrong, maybe they were right. I wouldn't know. In the church where the service was held I prayed that they would, one day, wake up from this sleep into a world, a rose garden, their dreams fulfilled.

At that point in time I didn't know I was praying for so many others too....

I wept until I felt nothing but complete emptiness inside.

On the fourth day I left along with Vijay and Vinny. I said my goodbyes and hugged Kmie U Flin. I held her for a long time, knowing I would never see her again.

42

ALMOST HALF WAY to Guwahati is the tiny village of Nongpoh. Once you leave the hills of Shillong and its surrounding areas and dip into smaller valleys and lower hills you stumble upon this town with its busy eating places and shops crammed on either side, jostling for space. I was startled to see the hermaphrodite in the first stall. Kong It (as we had always called him) had been there since my school days and didn't seem to have aged much. We were all famished and Vinny and Vijay strode without hesitation to the nearest tea shop—a wooden shack painted black with mobile oil and a black tin roof but fronted with the most gorgeous array of flower pots, bursting with colour. The steps were of rough stone almost casually put together, they shook wearily as we stepped into the dhaba filled with smoke and morning sunbeams. I strolled in casually with them and sat on a bench long enough for three, the table wide enough for six but pushed against a window with a view of the rolling hills outside.

Then I saw him in the next table. The sun slanted on his leucoderma face, lighting up his eyes that looked silently outwards. He was strumming his guitar and singing a Bob Dylan song?

Everyone wants to know why he couldn't adjust

Adjust to what—a dream that bust?

He was a clean cut kid

But they made a killer out of him

That's what they did.

They said what's up is down, they said what isn't is,

They put ideas in his head, he thought were his.

He was a clean cut kid

But they made a killer out of him

That's what they did.

"What a morbid song to sing early in the morning," Vinny grimaced eating a plate of noodles mixed with raw tomatoes, chillies and onions cut very small, Shillong style.

How would she know that for the singer there was no morning, no night, only bewildering hours inhabited by the spirits of slaughtered dreams. I remembered Robert and I stretched out my hand to touch him but he wasn't there.

They said, congratulations, you get what is takes

They sent him back to the rat race

Without any brakes

I stepped out into the ordinariness of a Wednesday morning. If I had turned back I would have met his eyes, but I didn't. I couldn't. Yet everything became clear to me like the opening of the Third eye.

Epilogue

THEY SAY THAT, like people, places and communities, countries and continents too have their karmas to go through.

Last year, four years after the tragedy, Aila suddenly arrived in Delhi without notice and said that she wanted to go to a place she had not been before.

In Jodhpur, leaning languidly, against the ramparts of the magnificent fort she told me that everything was much better now in Shillong. She told me without my asking. She knew as she always did what was, foremost, in my mind.

Everything and everyone?

Ho oid, she whispered. Yes.

And in that one word I found great comfort.

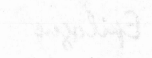